THE MISSING WITNESS MYSTERY

THE TED WILFORD SERIES

THE MISSING WITNESS MYSTERY

NORVIN PALLAS

WILDSIDE PRESS

CHAPTER 1

A NARROW ESCAPE

THE SIGN on the door of the office read "Closed," but the door was unlocked and the light was on. Christopher Dobson, the crusty editor of the Forestdale *Town Crier*, could be plainly seen through the large plate-glass window. Ted Wilford pushed the door open, and the editor looked up.

"No luck, Ted?" he asked, reading the answer from Ted's air of defeat.

"No, just a false alarm." Ted placed the car keys on the editor's desk, then dropped into a chair opposite him. "You can't blame the correspondent who phoned in the tip. There *was* a strong resemblance—I mean, if you were looking for it. But this man had lived there for years—including the time Lafferton was in prison—and his neighbors all vouch for him."

The possibility that a criminal who was the object of a nationwide search had found his way to their area was exciting, but extremely unlikely. Otherwise, Ted reflected, he would never have been given the assignment, for Carl Allison, the paper's full-time reporter, handled all the important stories that *had* to be done. Ted, college student and part-time cub reporter, was given either the smaller stories or those that seemed unlikely to develop. Nevertheless he welcomed these chances, for they interrupted the regular routine of answering the phone, typing stories and running errands. And there was always the possibility that the big story would come his way someday.

"You haven't heard from your friend yet?" asked the editor.

"No. Marty wasn't sure just which bus he would catch and I wasn't sure how long I'd be working, so we arranged to meet here."

Mr. Dobson tapped his pipe on his ash tray, and Ted knew that a story was coming. The editor enjoyed reminiscing, but only when there was an appreciative listener like Ted. Usually there was little time for it, but on Saturday afternoons the pace sometimes slowed down, telephone calls were fewer and that sign on the door kept out all except the most determined visitors.

Mr. Dobson's tale involved an important man—he didn't give his name—who had been arrested for some minor violation and asked the editor not to print the story.

"He pointed out to me that it was just a small story—only an inch or two—and why should his reputation be wrecked just for the sake of other people's idle curiosity? Surely he had a right to his privacy."

Taking a few puffs on his pipe, Mr. Dobson continued:

"I told him that he had sacrificed his right to privacy when he broke the law, but he answered that so far he hadn't been found guilty, although he didn't claim he was innocent. We both knew differently. However, guilty or innocent, the matter became of public concern as soon as there was sufficient evidence to bring him to trial. That seemed unfair to him, but I explained that unless newspapers were free to report on our legal processes, the public would have no means of judging whether these processes were operating fairly. There might even be occasions when he would want newspaper help in locating witnesses, for instance. Or perhaps, while technically guilty, he might feel that the law was unfair or being unjustly applied, and want to rally public support. None of these things could happen without a free press.

"He seemed to feel I ought to suppress the story as a personal favor, but I told him if I did it for him I would have to do it for other persons, too. Then what confidence would people have in the paper? And even though he hoped to plead guilty and have a quiet trial, I pointed out that it would be difficult to keep such a thing covered up. If his friends heard he was arrested but read nothing about it in the paper, they might even think he had been guilty of something much more serious than he actually was. On the other hand, as long as the paper printed the story, it wouldn't be necessary for him to make any explanations."

"How did he take it?" Ted inquired.

"Oh, I think he finally saw the justice of my arguments, but still felt that somehow he ought to be an exception. It's more difficult to apply these things to yourself than to other people."

As the editor leaned back once more there was a sudden hissing of air brakes outside. He and Ted turned to look out, but Ted could not see the street very well from where he sat.

"A dog," the editor reported after a moment. "He tried to cross that busy street, and wouldn't have made it if the truck hadn't peeled some of the rubber off its tires. Well, he seems to be all right and he's trotting along on his way."

"No one in the truck hurt from stopping so suddenly?"

"Apparently not. The driver's going on now. It's a funny thing, but those screeching brakes brought everybody on the street to attention. Probably no one knows that dog, but just for a moment there everybody was worried about him."

Ted relaxed for a few moments longer. There was work he could have done but he was expecting Marty at any moment. He looked at his watch. It was growing a little late. Maybe it would have been wiser to meet Marty at the bus depot, but if he were to go there now he might miss him on the way.

Marty Blaine was an upperclassman and Ted had just finished his freshman year, but they had become friends anyway. When Ted learned that Marty would be visiting his aunt near Forestdale during the summer, he invited him to stop off for a visit.

Ted's back was to the door, and so he did not see Marty approach, but Mr. Dobson did.

"I think your friend's starting to leave, Ted," he said. "You'd better catch him."

Ted ran out to find Marty walking away uncertainly.

"That sign on the door confused me," said Marty with a laugh. "I thought I must have misunderstood you."

"That's just to keep out the public," Ted explained, steering Marty back toward the office door. "Here, let me take your bag." Ted reached for it, and Marty protested but allowed Ted to take it from his hand. And then Ted very nearly dropped it, for the unexpected weight caught him by surprise.

"Say, what have you got in there?" he asked.

"Just a few gold bricks. I prefer them to travelers' checks."

By this time they were inside the office. "I'd like you to meet Martin Blaine, Mr. Dobson," Ted said and they shook hands. "Do I have time to show him around, Mr. Dobson, or are you in a hurry to lock up?"

"No hurry at all, Ted. Take all the time you like." The telephone rang just then and the editor turned away.

Ted led Marty about the office, showing him their files, dummies and other things he thought would interest him. Marty had studied journalism, although he did not intend to make a career of it, and asked many questions.

"Of course this isn't a very big paper," Ted explained, "so maybe it won't tell you everything you'd like to know."

"No, Ted, I think somehow you might learn more here than you could touring a big plant. Here you can see the whole picture. It's a weekly, isn't it?"

"No, semi-weekly with about three thousand circulation."

"Three thousand?" Marty whistled. "That's just about the population of the town, isn't it?"

"Almost. That doesn't mean one paper for everybody, of course— that would be too much to expect. But we have quite a circulation in the rural areas around here and even in some nearby towns that have no paper of their own. Come on in the back and I'll show you the printing plant."

The printer and his assistant had gone home for the day, so they had the larger back room to themselves.

"And a good thing, too," Ted remarked. "Mr. White wouldn't care much about having us loitering around here while he was working. He's all business—come right in and go right out."

"Do I smell printer's ink?"

"That's it," said Ted with satisfaction. "That's the thing you miss when you get away from here. And if you do miss it, that means you're hooked. You're doomed to be a newspaperman."

"You've pretty well decided, haven't you, Ted?"

"What other kinds of jobs *are* there?" asked Ted with a grin. "I'll be on some newspaper if I have anything to say about it, but maybe not this one. That will depend on a lot of things."

"Do you prefer a large paper or a small one?"

"I don't know, Marty," said Ted thoughtfully. "My brother Ronald decided in favor of a big newspaper, but Ken Kutler—he's our rival reporter up on the North Ridge *News-Record*—wouldn't work on anything except a small one. I guess it depends on how you're cut out."

"You make more money on a big paper, don't you?"

"Yes, you earn more," Ted admitted, "but you spend more, too. Oh, I suppose it's satisfying to feel you're reaching so many readers, but Ken says you just get lost in the shuffle."

"But what sort of stories do you handle here, Ted? Isn't most of your work concerned with small things like parties and trips and weddings—things too small to interest a large paper?"

"Oh, I suppose so, though we get our share of excitement, too. I think I would be very happy someday in a job like Mr. Dobson's—but first I'd have to feel sure I was qualified for it."

They had completed their tour of the printing room, and Marty asked, "Is this all?"

"Just about. We've got some storage room in the basement, and there's a dusty attic room for our old files. Every so often I have to go up there for something, and get my ears full of cobwebs. Now, are you about ready for dinner?"

"If I were any more ready, I might be too weak to get there. You're sure it's all right with your mother, Ted?"

"Oh, sure. If she heard you were out this way and hadn't stopped, she'd have been hurt. I don't know, though—that suitcase is pretty heavy, and I live on the edge of town. What would you say if I called up Nelson and had him drive us home? He wouldn't mind."

"Oh, no, Ted, don't bother. I don't mind. In fact I'd like to see a little more of the town. My aunt's farm is about forty miles south of here and I used to spend part of each summer with her, but I never came through Forestdale before. And I think we can manage my suitcase between us—if I don't find someone to buy my gold bricks en route."

Ted called his mother to let her know they were on their way. Then they said good night to Mr. Dobson and started for home. They walked slowly, Ted carrying the heavy bag. He pointed out the local sights and Marty asked questions.

"Did you see the little dog that almost got hit?" asked Ted in his turn.

"Oh, yes, I was standing a little way down the street—State Street, isn't it?—when it happened. A little white curly-haired puppy.

It gave him a good scare. I suppose he had the idea that the world is just a big, friendly place. I don't think he'll believe it's quite so friendly after this."

"Well, I suppose a puppy hasn't any business wandering around these heavily traveled streets on a Saturday afternoon."

At the Wilford home, Mrs. Wilford came in from the kitchen to greet them and to be introduced to the visitor.

"Dinner in fifteen minutes," she informed them, as Ted led Marty upstairs.

He put the suitcase down in Ronald's old room. "There's an empty dresser there if you want to unpack some of your things."

"Oh, I don't think I'll bother unpacking just for one night."

"What would you like to do tonight, Marty? Nelson will be over. We could go to a movie, or invite some of the fellows over—anything you want."

"You sure you guys don't have dates for tonight?"

"No, not tonight. There's a little party tomorrow night, but I suppose you'll miss that if you really have to go."

"Yes, Ted, I want to get to the farm before dark. But if you're sure it's up to me, I'll tell you the truth. I'm tired from traveling. I'd just as soon sit around tonight and chew the fat a little, if you don't mind."

"No, that'll be all right with us. Anything I can get you before I go?"

"Oh, no, everything seems just fine here. I'll be ready for dinner in fifteen minutes, all right. That smells like hamburgers cooking."

From his own room, Ted could hear Marty moving around the other room a little. The fleeting thought came to him that Marty hadn't opened that heavy suitcase while he was still in the room.

CHAPTER 2

A CONFIDENCE—ALMOST

AS HE HAD PROMISED, Nelson Morgan came over later. He had spent most of the day helping a neighbor to move, using a rented trailer, but was ready for action just the same. When he learned that Ted and Marty intended to spend the evening just sitting and talking, he was flabbergasted.

"You mean, just sit around and not do anything?"

"Why, sure, what's wrong with that?" asked Ted, winking at Marty.

"Because you can't do it, that's why. You've got to be doing *something*."

"Oh, we'll be doing something. We'll be thinking."

"I mean something with your muscles."

"He means he'd rather use the muscles in his legs than the muscles in his head," said Marty, jokingly.

"I'm not sure I've got any muscles in my head," Nelson retorted. However, when he became convinced that the other two really did not care for either a movie or a drive or an evening swim, he became reconciled to the idea.

"At least we can watch television. There's a good mystery and . . ."

"No television," Ted informed him. "Mom's having some visitors, too, and they'll have the living room. We're confined to the kitchen."

Nelson looked crestfallen. "I'd ask you over to my place, but Ted knows how big a family I've got. The only place we could talk would be in my dark room. But look, we've got to do *something*."

Ted thought that this might not be such a bad idea, even though Marty had claimed to be tired, so he suggested Monopoly.

"I haven't played that for years," Marty recalled.

"Me, either," Nelson put in.

Ted went off to find the game, which was dusty from years of neglect. He also brought out pop and pretzels, and Nelson cheered up. The others set up the game and they were ready to play.

The game moved along in a desultory way as they talked over the past year at college.

"Anyone ever have Professor Porter?" asked Marty, as Nelson landed on Boardwalk bringing the game to a close.

"We're both getting him next year," Ted replied.

"Well, when you do, be sure you tell him you like Brahms' *Fourth Symphony* better than his *First*. He'll think you're a real connoisseur. I expect that's how I got such a good grade from him. I wonder what Brahms' *Fourth Symphony* sounds like?"

"How come you said you liked it when you had never heard it?" asked Nelson, puzzled, for Marty was no bluffer.

"I guess my thoughts must have wandered. I thought he was talking about Tschaikovsky."

About eleven o'clock, Nelson said: "You know what? This is just about the best time for listening to police calls. Why don't we sit out in the car awhile and see what we can pick up?"

"I guess that's as good a way as any to cool off," Marty agreed.

"Unless there's a robbery nearby; then things might get too hot," Ted added.

However, nothing very exciting came over the air for some time. Forestdale was a small town and their own neighborhood was in one of the quietest sections of the community, so there was little to expect. Forestdale had only one police car on duty at any given time with another in reserve, and sometimes this one car was called out of town by arrangement with nearby communities. The boys heard one call for an ambulance, another call for a suspected prowler which turned out to be a man who had forgotten his key, and this seemed to be about as much excitement as they could expect, even on a Saturday night.

Suddenly the voice of the dispatcher came on again. "Be on the lookout for license number LU-815, repeat LU-815. The late-model blue sedan is registered in the name of Grover Hale. He is a bank teller for the Stantonville State Bank in Stanton, and is wanted for questioning in connection with a shortage discovered by bank examiners this afternoon. It is believed that he may pass through Forestdale. Approach the car with circumspection. He is not known to be dangerous, but he may be desperate. License number LU-815. That is all."

"Well!" Marty exclaimed. "I hope he didn't get my twenty-five bucks. I've got an account there."

"Then maybe you've seen the man," Ted offered.

"No, I've never actually been in the bank. My uncle started a savings account for me as a gift when I graduated from high school. That makes it more than twenty-five dollars—three years interest on top of it. Maybe we ought to go after this thief and see if he's got my money."

"I doubt that it would have your name on it even if we did catch him," Nelson replied.

"I suppose there's no real loss as long as deposits are insured," Ted observed, "but I imagine a thing like this hurts the bank anyway. A lot of people may decide they're dealing with an institution that isn't very reliable, and take their business elsewhere."

"Why do they call it the Stantonville State Bank?" Nelson inquired. "It makes it sound like a real small-time outfit."

"I suppose they want to emphasize what an old institution it is, going back to the days when Stanton was still a village," Marty explained. "Anyway, I guess I won't have to stay awake worrying over my twenty-eight dollars, or whatever it is," he added with a laugh.

His friends laughed with him, but it occurred to Ted to wonder about Marty. Was he rich or poor? Ted had known him for nearly a year, but had never thought about it before. He did know Marty was an orphan, under the care of a guardian until he was twenty-one and that he had little in the way of home life. Suppose this particular bank was not insured; would a loss of twenty-eight dollars mean very much to him? He had laughed about it, so apparently it didn't.

"Well, I don't think I'd want to lose twenty-five dollars," Nelson decided, "even if it wasn't a matter of life or death. It's the principle of the thing."

"Plus the interest," said Ted.

"I suppose when it comes down to it, everybody's got money troubles," said Marty thoughtfully. "If you haven't got enough, you worry how to get it. If you have got enough, you worry that some-body will get it away from you."

"Whoever has enough?" asked Nelson.

"Oh, I suppose some people have enough money to buy every-thing they really want," Ted declared, "but they have to worry about how to invest the rest. I admit that's a nicer kind of worry, though, than worrying how you're going to meet the grocery bill."

"I suppose the police'll catch up with this Grover Hale before very long," Nelson observed, "and I won't say I'm sorry about it. But somehow running off with the bank's money that way doesn't seem as bad as holding up a bank with a gun. At least nobody was in danger of getting shot."

"In some ways it's worse," Marty put in. "Nobody has any con-fidence in a bank robber, but an embezzler is a person whom people trusted and he violated their trust. The worst of it is that he can usu-ally get away with a lot more than a bank robber can, because he can keep coming back for more."

"Want to scout around and see if we can spot the car?" Nelson suggested, still intent upon some action.

But his friends declined.

"Hale may be hundreds of miles away from here by now," Marty pointed out, "if he ever came this way. It seems to me that if he thought the police were looking for him around Forestdale, he would be sure to go somewhere else."

"Anyway, what can we do that the police aren't doing?" Ted shrugged. "And I don't know what we'd do with him even if we found him."

"Arrest him," said Nelson determinedly. "Ever hear of a citizen's arrest?"

"Pretty tricky, and nothing I'd care to get involved in if I could help it." Ted yawned and stretched.

"Let's call it a night," Marty suggested, and Nelson finally gave up.

"All right, then, miss out on all the fun. You'll be sorry."

"What are you going to do?" Ted inquired.

"Go home to bed. What did you think?" He explained to Marty, "My mother never worries about me as long as I'm with Ted. She doesn't know him as well as she thinks."

Mrs. Wilford had retired and Ted and Marty went directly upstairs. They said good night, and Ted went on to his own room where he sat down on the bed and yawned and stretched for a while before taking off his shoes. Then Marty knocked on his door.

"Ted, this is a silly thing to bother you about, but do you have a telephone number where you can call for the weather report? If it should rain tomorrow, I may want to call my aunt and change plans for meeting her."

"Sure, Marty." Ted gave him the number. "But wait, I can call for you."

"Oh, never mind. I can handle it myself."

The Wilfords did not have an extension telephone but their regular phone was the plug-in type, and Ted could have brought it upstairs to his room. However, his mother would be up early and might want to use it, so he had not done so. With his bedroom door still open, he could hear Marty's voice downstairs. Odd, he thought. There was no use talking to the weather reporter who was on tape.

When Marty came back upstairs, Ted went to the doorway.

"Get it all right?"

"What? Oh, sure, sure."

"Well, what's the weather outlook?"

"Oh, thunder showers tonight and overcast and scattered showers through tomorrow. I'll have to see how it looks tomorrow, before calling my aunt."

"We get the Stanton paper in the morning," Ted pointed out. "Maybe that would give you a better idea of the weather down that way than our local report. Their coverage is more comprehensive."

"Thanks, but it isn't that important."

"I thought I heard you talking downstairs," Ted remarked. "Have trouble getting the number?"

"Yes, I must have dialed wrong and the operator came on. But she put me through all right. Well, good night again, Ted."

Having put in a very full day, Ted fell asleep almost at once. But whether it was the humid night, or the approaching storm, he must have felt uneasy for his sleep was filled with dreams. At one time he thought he heard movement in the next room, but somehow it blended in with his dream and he did not awaken right away. When he did, it was with a start. A bright flash of lightning swept through the room, followed some seconds later by distant rolling thunder. He sat up in bed.

Was it the storm which had awakened him, or was it something else? He listened carefully. Then he was sure. There was someone moving about in the kitchen which was directly below his room. And the noise that had awakened him? Surely it was the closing of the back door.

Quietly he pulled on his robe and stepped into his slippers. Making his way noiselessly through the darkened hall, he crept down the stairs. There was a light in the kitchen. Approaching the doorway, Ted saw Marty standing in the middle of the room apparently lost in thought. The visitor was still fully dressed, and in Ted's mind there was no question but that he had just come in from outside.

No longer attempting to be quiet Ted strode into the room, and Marty looked up quickly.

"Oh, Ted, I'm awfully sorry if I awakened you. I didn't want to bother anyone."

"That's all right, but you should have let me know if anything was wrong. I could have put a ventilating fan in your room if it was too warm."

"Nothing was wrong, Ted. I just seemed to have trouble falling asleep. Maybe it's this storm." He looked at Ted speculatively, as though wondering how much Ted knew. "I like storms. There is something exciting about them. I stepped out for a few minutes to watch this one moving in. It's rather spectacular, approaching over that ridge of hills."

"Thunder Mountain." Ted nodded. "That's where its name came from. What would you say to a sandwich, Marty?"

"Really, no, Ted. I'm not hungry."

"But we may as well have something. If Mom hears us, she'll think we just got up for something to eat."

Ted made some sandwiches and tried to show he had no intention of prying into Marty's moods or problems. Still, it was obvious to him that something was weighing on Marty's mind, and Marty must have realized that he knew.

"Ted," he said, in a sudden rush of confidence, "I don't want to be mysterious or anything. It's just that it's very difficult for me to unburden myself to a friend."

"What are friends for, if you can't talk to them?"

"I know. That's the way it ought to be, but it's different with me. I was raised all alone, you know, and my guardian—well, I just never had anybody I could talk to. And this time it's especially hard, because it really isn't my problem. It's someone else's. You understand, don't you?"

"I think so, Marty. I know you're worrying about something that probably isn't any of my business, unless you want to make it my business. But if there is any way I could help you, you know I would."

"I'm sure of that, Ted," said Marty. "But this is something I know you couldn't do anything about. Thanks anyway."

They finished their sandwiches, and went upstairs.

"Good night, Ted—this time for real," and with a smile Marty closed his door.

CHAPTER 3

RIVALS WORK TOGETHER

THE STORM had passed by morning, and the sun rose in a cloudless sky with the air a little cooler than before. Evidently the weatherman had been mistaken when he predicted an overcast and threatening day.

Both boys were anxious to read about the Stantonville Bank affair. The story gave many more details than they had obtained over the police radio, though there was careful hedging. The report constantly used the word "alleged," and was very careful not to make a direct accusation concerning Grover Hale. As a newspaperman, Ted recognized the necessity of avoiding any possible grounds for libel, so a newspaper had to be less frank than the police radio which had said quite bluntly that Hale was being sought for questioning in connection with the embezzlement. The newspaper account merely stated the teller had left for his regular vacation and was being requested to return for any help he might be able to give the police. However, the careful newspaper reader was not likely to be fooled by this wording, and it was clear that Grover Hale was the principal suspect.

Many of the details were confusing to the two boys since the affair concerned matters of bank records and procedures which were Greek to them. But a state of confusion also existed at the bank, and until a careful audit of the records was made it would not be known how the embezzlement had been handled or how much was missing.

"I read of one case," said Marty, laughing, "where the police had to bring the thief back to the bank to straighten out the records, because no one else could do it."

"Well, I'd just as soon not be in Grover Hale's shoes," Ted decided. "They seem pretty certain he headed north toward Forestdale, though."

"That was *his* story. The chances are that he's down in New Orleans by this time."

In the afternoon Marty suggested that they walk to Thunder Mountain, and was surprised to learn that it was ten miles away. On a clear day, many strangers in Forestdale were deceived in the same way. But the boys did take a short walk in that direction. Upon returning, they played some records and Marty looked over Ted's and his brother's books.

"Take along anything you want," Ted invited. "It's going to be a long summer."

"No thanks, Ted. I don't know when I could return them."

"We'll see you at school in the fall."

"I hope so, Ted, though if I can work things out, you'll see me before then. Would it be all right if I manage to stop off on my way home for a longer visit?"

"Fine, Marty. I'll look forward to it."

Marty frowned: "I didn't say for *sure*, Ted. It will depend on how things turn out for me. But I will if I can. Maybe I'll have a chance to tag along with you on your newspaper rounds for a day or two."

"You might find it pretty dull," said Ted with a laugh. "There's a lot of routine stuff between the exciting happenings."

"I'll take my chances on that. I think I'd find even the routine exciting, at least for a while."

"Why don't I call Nelson and let him drive you down to your aunt's?" asked Ted as it neared the time for Marty to leave. "I'm sure he wouldn't mind a drive of forty miles."

"Forty miles for me, but that would be eighty for you," Marty pointed out. "No, I don't want to bother him. The bus will be almost as fast, and anyway I know you've got a party coming up this evening."

"I wish you could have stayed for that, Marty. I'd like you to have met some of the crowd."

"I know, Ted," said Marty. "Maybe we can work it out the next time I'm here."

Ted walked with Marty to the bus station, for he refused to accept a ride from Nelson for even this short trip. Ted helped carry that heavy suitcase once again, and reflected that he hadn't yet been allowed to see inside it. There was only a short wait, and then Marty got on his bus. When the bus pulled out, Ted turned away and walked home slowly. He had a sudden hunch that Marty would not be back that summer unless he somehow managed to solve the problem which was so obviously worrying him.

The party was fun. After dropping off their dates, Nelson drove Ted back to his house and they stood for a few minutes talking by the car.

"That embezzlement's something, isn't it?" Nelson exclaimed. "I wish we could have found Grover Hale. If we had recovered the money, it would have been a really big story for you, wouldn't it?"

"I guess so," Ted agreed. "I haven't heard anything about a reward, though."

"Who said anything about a reward?" demanded Nelson, who had been thinking about that very thing.

"Nobody," Ted returned, grinning.

"I wonder where he is now? Where would you go if everybody thought you were going north?"

"Marty said he would go south, but it seems to me I'd go east or west."

"That's because you're too shrewd, Ted. I don't think robbers are that clever. But I don't think the police are very shrewd, either. If a robber says he's going north, where do they look for him? North, of course."

"What else can they do? If they've got a clue, they have to follow it up. Maybe it's phony most of the time, but once in a while it pans out. If they didn't follow up their clues, then they wouldn't have a starting point at all."

"Well, maybe so," Nelson agreed reluctantly. "I'll tell you something about this business, though. I've been listening to a few more police calls, and I think they know pretty definitely that Grover Hale came north. Maybe his car was spotted, or something. You sure you don't want to look for him?"

"Look, son, I'm beat, and Monday is my busy morning. See me about it after they post a reward. Anyway," Ted went on more cordially, "if you were going to look for him, where would you begin?"

"I don't know. Just drive around, I guess, and see if we could spot his car."

"Don't you think he knows by now that the police are after him? He won't be cruising around in *that* car, you can be sure of that."

"Maybe he'd have to. It's probably the only car he's got, and if he tried to steal one it might pinpoint him for the police."

"More likely he's holed up somewhere and I don't think it would be in Forestdale. This is too small a town to get lost in."

"Maybe he rented a car. Couldn't we at least check the car rental agencies?"

"Probably the very first thing the police did. You don't really think they're stupid, do you?"

"Maybe not, but if anybody's going to collect that reward, I'd like to be the one. What good does it do the police? They're not allowed to take a reward anyway. And I've got my eye on a honey of a foreign camera. It's . . ."

"Good night, chum!" Ted exclaimed, knowing that if he once let Nelson get started talking about cameras he might not get to bed for hours.

Mr. Dobson brought up the matter of the bank embezzlement the first thing next morning.

"Ted, I know you've heard about this Stantonville State Bank thing, and that Grover Hale supposedly either came to Forestdale, or passed through Forestdale on Saturday afternoon. I've just called the police station and it seems a good many people called in, claiming they saw the car here. How about getting along to the station to see what you can pick up? I want to know the names of the witnesses and just what they claim they saw. Of course even if they did see Hale he may have gone on from here, and there won't be any story for us unless he is apprehended in our area. But see what you think about it."

"Sure thing," said Ted eagerly. "Do you want me to go out and interview these witnesses?"

"Use your own judgment about that, Ted. I'm afraid that I can't let you have my car this morning since I'll be out myself. Some of the witnesses may be too far away for you to reach on foot. If so, there's probably no hurry. There won't be any story for us this morning. You can either interview them by telephone or wait till I get back."

Ted left quickly for the nearby station house. Of course he knew why he had been given the assignment instead of Carl Allison. When

Mr. Dobson said, "There won't be any story for us this morning," that explained everything. He was being given one of the long shots.

Ted was not exactly surprised to recognize Ken Kutler's car pulled up in the "reserve" space in front of the police station. Forestdale was not far off Ken's regular beat, and the *Town Crier* and the *News-Record* staged a continuous battle for circulation, advertising and stories. The competition had been friendly while Ted's brother Ronald was the chief reporter for the *Town Crier*, but Carl Allison and Ken Kutler were bitter rivals.

Ted found Ken just about ready to leave the station.

"I suppose you're here on this bank story, Ted—or did a bigger story break? I'm always afraid to pick up a copy of the *Town Crier* for fear I'll read about an earthquake I slept through."

"No, nothing bigger than the bank thing," Ted admitted.

"I've got a list of the witnesses who were supposed to have seen Hale's car, and I'm going to interview them. I see you're on foot. Want to come along with me?" Ken offered.

"Fine, but I'd better get briefed at the desk first."

"Oh, don't bother. I'll brief you on the way."

Ted was glad of the chance to interview the witnesses directly instead of over the telephone. And the witnesses would feel less annoyed at giving their story just once, instead of repeating it for each reporter. Then, too, Ted would get the benefit of Ken's careful questioning—and perhaps could contribute something himself. Two heads are better than one—"unless they're on the same animal," as Nelson once remarked.

"What about these witnesses?" asked Ted. "Did they really see the car?"

"Apparently so," said Ken, frowning. "Of course you know how witnesses are—some are more reliable than others, and even the most reliable may differ on details. That's something we'll have to try and judge, and I'm counting on you to help me there. I've got a bad habit of being skeptical about everything anyone tells me."

"What do the police think?"

"Well, they're not saying exactly what they think. They have already interviewed all these witnesses—either directly or by telephone. I haven't seen the reports of what the witnesses said, but that's all right with me. I'd rather interview them myself and get my own impressions."

"Where was the car seen?"

"Apparently on State Street, near Orange Avenue. At least that is what most of the witnesses say, the desk sergeant informed me."

"That's less than a block from the *Town Crier* office," said Ted thoughtfully. "Are they sure it's the right car?"

"Well, Ted, you know how it is when you're dealing with eyewitnesses. In the first place, most people heard the description over the police radio, or they heard about it from somebody who heard the police broadcast, or they heard the news bulletins late Saturday night or on Sunday or they read about it in the Sunday paper. Now obviously they *think* they saw the right car, or they wouldn't have telephoned in. I'll tell you one thing, though. None of the reports said what kind of car it was but I've been informed that it was a Pontiac. The police like to hold back a little of their information, in order to test the reliability of witnesses. If the witness says it was a Pontiac, it will be a point in his favor."

"How many witnesses are there?"

"Ten altogether—six women and four men. I'm going first to see Mrs. Hartley and Mrs. Collins. They are sisters, who live together, so we can kill two birds with one stone. All but two of the witnesses live in or near Forestdale. I don't know about the other two—we may not have time to reach them this morning. I've got a deadline, too, you know. But we'll go as far as we can."

"I don't want to interfere with your assignment," Ted told him. "Do you want me to speak up at these interviews?"

"Say anything you want to, Ted. There's no use standing there like a statue. I'll sort of take the lead, though. Just one caution—be careful not to put any ideas in their heads. Let them say exactly what they saw or think they saw. You know a lot of people have a tendency to say whatever they think the listener wants to hear. And if these witnesses are like most witnesses, we're going to have trouble enough sifting through their statements to find out the truth. Well, here's the first stop."

CHAPTER 4

TOO MANY WITNESSES

IT WAS MRS. HARTLEY who answered their ring. She knew Ted by sight and Ken by reputation, and so was glad to answer their questions. Mrs. Collins was also at home, so they were able to interview them together.

"You say that you both saw this car the police are looking for, and you saw it on Saturday afternoon on State Street," Ken began, after they were all seated in the living room.

"Yes," Mrs. Hartley affirmed.

"Just where on State Street was it?"

"Just the other side of Orange Avenue—not far from the newspaper office," she added, turning to Ted.

"Do you know about what time it was?"

"I think . . ." She hesitated. "It must have been about a quarter to four."

"Almost four o'clock," Mrs. Collins corrected. "I know we were later getting home than we expected we would be."

"Could you describe the car for me?"

"Well," said Mrs. Hartley thoughtfully, "it was a blue coupe, just like the car the police mentioned."

"I thought it was more a blue-green," Mrs. Collins amended.

"Would you know what kind of car it was?"

"You mean the make?" asked Mrs. Hartley. "I'm afraid neither my sister nor I know very much about cars."

"Do you have any idea of the year?"

"Well, I think it was a pretty new car—but not a real new one, like this year's model."

"About three or four years old," Mrs. Collins added. "Unless it was well taken care of. Then it might be older than that."

"I see," said Ken, nodding agreeably. Ted knew that it was a good idea never to disagree with a witness.

"Now, of course," Ken went on, "there is fairly heavy traffic on State Street on Saturday afternoon. How did you happen to notice this car? What was there about it that attracted your attention?"

"Why, I don't suppose we would have noticed it at all if it hadn't been for the dog," said Mrs. Hartley thoughtfully.

"A dog?" Ted exclaimed involuntarily. Then he immediately subsided, leaving the interviewing to Ken.

"You say there was a dog?" asked Ken, to whom this appeared to be a new piece of information. "Was the dog in the car?"

"Oh, no, not in the car. He was crossing State Street and this car almost hit him."

"The blue car almost hit the dog?"

"Oh, no. The blue coupe was parked at the curb. It was a truck going by that almost hit the dog. I was just talking to Dorothy about—oh, well, something about our shopping that I'm sure wouldn't interest you one bit, and there was a sudden screaming of brakes. I don't mean the kind of screaming that an ordinary car's brakes make, but more like the sound of compressed air. It was enough to scare the wits out of a person. We looked up, of course, and we saw the truck coming to a sudden stop. It swerved a little, too, and I thought maybe it was going to hit the blue coupe at the curb, but it didn't. We were afraid that a child might have been hit, but then we saw a white dog walking across the street as though nothing had happened. It looked like a show dog, possibly very valuable."

"It was just a mongrel," said Mrs. Collins with a sniff. "And he wasn't all white—he had brown spots. Probably a stray. I don't think he had a collar on. At least I didn't see a collar. I don't think people would let a valuable show dog wander through busy traffic."

"A dog can sneak out before anyone realizes what has happened," said Mrs. Hartley quickly. "And the weather Saturday was very fine, you know—doors would be open, and some dogs can push open a screen door."

"But you don't think the dog had anything to do with the blue coupe, do you?" Ken went on.

"Oh, no, I don't think so. But of course we noticed the coupe after it was almost hit by the truck. You wonder how people are going to react after they've almost been struck."

"They?" asked Ted alertly.

"Oh, yes. There were two of them. Didn't you know that?"

"There were two men in the blue car?" asked Ken carefully.

"Of course. Well—I suppose I shouldn't exactly say that. There was the driver and a young man just getting out of the car. The door was open and he was lifting his suitcase from the car. He was frozen in that position for a few moments when the interruption came—we all were. Then when everybody saw that everything was all right, the young man laughed and pulled his suitcase all the way out of the car, thanked the driver and walked away. And that was the last we saw of him."

"Did you get a good look at the driver? Which side of the street were you on?"

"On the side where the newspaper office is, the same side the car was parked on. But I couldn't tell you much about the driver. We could see him through the windshield, but we were a little farther down the street and he was leaning over, talking to the young man. Then as the brakes screamed, he turned around the other way to look. By the time we came up to them, the young man was walking ahead of us and the car was getting ready to pull away."

"Could you describe this young man?"

"Well, I really didn't see very much of him, either, since his back was turned to us. I think he was tall, nicely built, wearing a business suit and carrying this rather heavy suitcase. He must have been about twenty-five years old."

"A little older than that," her sister interposed. "At least twenty-eight. Maybe thirty."

"I see. Just to make the picture a little clearer, which way was the dog crossing the street?"

"I really don't know much about directions, but it was from our side of the street to the other."

"No, from the south to the north," Mrs. Collins corrected. "That's the way he started, but the truck frightened him, so he turned around and went back the other way."

"Well, maybe he did," Mrs. Hartley agreed. "I just saw him going off on the other side."

"I don't suppose it really matters. Did you notice the truck particularly, or the driver?"

"Well, no, just that it was a big red truck. We could only see the top of it because it was on the other side of the blue coupe, but I did notice the driver sort of wiping off his forehead, as though relieved that he hadn't struck either the dog or the car. Then he drove on."

"Is there anything more you can tell me about the blue car? You didn't get the license number?"

"No, not for sure. I remember glancing at it, and when the news bulletin came in it sounded a little like it, so we thought it best to call the police."

"Why should we get it?" the other sister broke in. "We know you should always try to get the license number if there's an accident, but this time there wasn't any accident. The truck driver must have been very alert, or he might not have avoided it."

"And anything more about the young man? You didn't notice where he went?"

"No," Mrs. Collins continued. "We turned into Marvin's Department Store right there and naturally we didn't bother looking for him after we came out."

"But would you know him if you should see him again? Could you identify him in court?"

"I think that probably I could," she affirmed.

"Oh, I don't think I would want to try," said Mrs. Hartley hastily. "I couldn't be sure, and I wouldn't want to take the risk of getting the wrong man in trouble."

Ken got to his feet, and the others followed his example. "I want to thank you ladies for helping us. If you should think of anything else, please call one of us."

"What will happen to those men if you find them?" asked Mrs. Hartley somewhat anxiously.

"I suppose the police will question them and if they haven't done anything that will be the end of it. But if this should develop into a big story, you can read about it in the *News-Record*."

"Or the *Town Crier*," said Ted with a laugh, and on this note they took their departure.

"Well, what did you think of our two witnesses?" asked Ken, when they had returned to the car.

"It's hard to say," said Ted thoughtfully. "They made a number of mistakes. I'm sure they're wrong about the time. It was twenty-five minutes after four when the incident with the dog happened. I know because I was at the *Town Crier* then, and Mr. Dobson looked out. And of course the dog couldn't have crossed the street from south to north. It would have to be east to west, or west to east. The car, too—they kept calling it a coupe, but it was a four-door sedan."

"I don't think that's very important, Ted, since they admitted they didn't know much about cars, and the word 'coupe' is a little ambiguous anyway. Which of the ladies would you rely on the most?"

"On Mrs. Hartley. She was being very careful about what she said. Mrs. Collins seemed to be waiting for her sister to say something so she could contradict it."

"You trust Mrs. Hartley, Ted, because you're a newspaperman and you've had some experience with witnesses. But if they were to appear in court, I'm afraid a jury would rely more heavily on Mrs. Collins. She has a forceful way of expressing herself, so that the jury would probably feel she knows what she's talking about. If you know someone personally, you can probably form a pretty good opinion of how reliable he is, but when you know him only slightly you may be fooled by superficial things. In all that sudden confusion, with the cars in front of them, do you really think Mrs. Collins could tell whether or not that dog had a collar on?"

"No, I don't, and that makes you wonder how reliable the rest of the information was." Ted considered. "Do you think it would help us any, Ken, if we could find that dog?"

"I doubt it. We're lucky about the dog, though, Ted. That's what focused everybody's attention on the car. Otherwise it would probably have gone unnoticed. Let's see who's next on our witness list. The closest address is Mr. Sheraton's, but . . ."

"That's Jim, who runs the barbershop. But it's closed on Mondays."

"Then we've got a good chance of finding him at home. Let's try."

Jim Sheraton was at home and willing to answer their questions. He had witnessed the incident through the large plate-glass window of his shop. He placed the time at four-fifteen, and he was able to identify the car both by make and year.

"What about the driver? Did you get a good look at him?" Ken inquired.

"No, I could hardly see him at all. But I did see this young man getting out of the car—or perhaps I should say boy. About eighteen, nineteen, twenty—around there. I saw him lifting something out of the car, but I couldn't tell from across the street what it was. I did wonder, though, why he carried it in the car instead of in the luggage compartment."

"Then did you notice where the young man went—or the car?"

"Oh, no, I couldn't stand around watching. I had work to do."

"What about other people in the shop with you?"

"There was my partner, but he had the inside chair. We each had customers in our chairs but they were facing away from the window at the moment, so I don't think they could have seen anything."

"What about customers waiting?"

"There were about two or three of them, but they didn't get up. I walked over to the window and told them that a dog had almost been hit, and they went back to their magazines."

This seemed to be all he could tell them so they thanked him and left.

The next woman had a really bizarre story to tell. She placed the scene of the near-accident about two blocks north of Orange Avenue, where it would obviously have been out of sight of the barbershop window. But she did notice the big red truck, the blue sedan and the young man getting out of the car.

"Of course I wouldn't have paid any attention," Miss Murphy went on, "if it hadn't been for the child. Ran right across the street in front of that big truck. It's a mercy the child wasn't killed. The truck was going slowly, and so the driver was fortunately able to stop. I don't know what parents are thinking of nowadays."

Ken and Ted exchanged startled glances. "A child, you say?" asked Ken.

"Why, yes, a small child, not more than five years old, I couldn't tell if it was a boy or girl—I really caught only a slight glimpse of him, you know. It was on the other side of the traffic and all."

Ken asked her further questions, but apparently she could be of no help in identifying either of the men in the car, nor did she know where the young man had gone or which direction the car had taken. Like the others, she had not noted the license number.

The next witness they called on, Mrs. Fromand, seemed to be even less reliable, although she spoke with a good deal of certainty. She had the time about right, but she placed the blue sedan on Orchid Lane, rather than on State Street, and she knew nothing about the accident with the dog and the red truck. But she did claim to have seen the driver getting out of the car.

"Could you describe him for us?" asked Ken.

"Well, I don't suppose I could tell you very much about him. He was a man of about forty-five, rather heavy, and outside of that there wasn't very much to notice about him."

"You say he was the driver. But is it possible that he was actually a passenger in the car, rather than the driver?"

"Now I don't know." She thought it over for a moment. "That's something that didn't occur to me. I didn't know there were two men involved. But I suppose he could have been a passenger. If he was, I didn't notice the driver, but I suppose he could have been leaning over, or something like that. I wasn't very close to them."

"Was there any particular reason why you noticed this car, Mrs. Fromand? Was there something about it that attracted your attention?"

"Yes, I thought he was parked rather close to a fire hydrant—there are no parking meters in Orchid Lane, you know. I had left my own car at home because I know how difficult it is to find a parking space on a Saturday afternoon. It annoyed me that I had had a rather long walk, and here was this man parked in a spot where I would not have dared to park."

The conversation continued for a few minutes more, but they were unable to elicit anything useful, so they thanked her and said good-by.

"That's half of them," Ted remarked, as they sat in the car writing in their notebooks.

"Yes, and let's hope the other half are more reliable than these," said Ken a little grimly, as he started the engine.

CHAPTER 5

UNRELIABILITY OF EYEWITNESSES

THEY WERE FORTUNATE in being able to reach the three other witnesses who lived or worked in Forestdale. The two men were at their jobs, but were not too busy to talk with them for a few minutes. The woman, who was a housewife, answered questions freely. Once again these stories differed in some of their details, though less so than the previous witnesses' accounts. With this accomplished, Ken drove Ted back to the newspaper office.

"That's all I can do for now, Ted. I've got a deadline to meet and I know you have, too. This afternoon when I have a little more time, I'll try to call the last two witnesses. If I'm able to reach them, I'll telephone you at home tonight to let you know what they say."

Ted got out of the car, knowing that Ken would do exactly as he promised. Even if he uncovered some startling fact from these last witnesses, Ted knew it would make no difference. Ken played hard, but he always played fair.

"Are you going to use this story in tomorrow's issue?" asked Ted in parting.

"What story?" said Ken with a growl, and drove off. Like Ted, he had been rather annoyed by the conflicting stories of the witnesses they had interviewed. You didn't expect two people to see things *exactly* alike, but how wrong could a person be?

Entering the office, Ted found the usual just-before-deadline rush on. Carl Allison was making some corrections for the printer, Miss Monroe was typing a last-minute story which had just come in, and Mr. Dobson was talking on the telephone with a proof sheet in front of him trying to rearrange the page in order to accommodate the new story. No one had time to pay much attention to Ted, although Mr. Dobson raised one eyebrow to ask if he had anything urgent to report, and Ted shook his head.

Then Carl asked him to take something back to the printer and bring back a proof. By the time Ted returned, he found Miss Monroe on the other telephone and she motioned him to take her chair and finish typing the story she had been copying. Two men had entered the office during Ted's brief absence, one an expressman and the other a stranger who seemed rather bewildered by his inability to get anyone's attention. Carl had to fill out a check to pay the expressman, which was ordinarily Mr. Dobson's job, for the editor—with the telephone caller still waiting—had gone to the file to look something up. To an outsider this would have looked rather hectic, but for the members of the newspaper staff it was their usual Monday morning routine.

Noon came, and the enemy—time—had been vanquished. The visitors had left the office, Carl and Miss Monroe had departed and Ted and Mr. Dobson were alone. Ted, with his notebook in front of him, gave Mr. Dobson the witnesses' different stories.

When he had finished, Mr. Dobson sat quietly for a few moments thinking the matter over. "Well, Ted," he said finally, "I can understand that you're put out about things—I believe this is the first time you've ever interviewed so many people about the same incident. Just the same, I hope you won't make the mistake of discounting *everything* these people said to you. The witnesses are either mistaken, or they are lying, and it is hard to see any reason why they should lie. But even a person who is deliberately lying will tell the truth about *most* things. After all, he is trying to get you to believe him and he lies only about the part that seems important to him. So I believe, Ted, that you will find a good deal of truth buried in these witnesses' statements."

"I suppose so," Ted agreed, "but how will I know it when I find it?"

Mr. Dobson laughed. "That's a good problem for you. Think it over at lunch. Are you meeting Nelson?"

"Yes. It's all right, isn't it, for me to talk it over with him? Maybe some idea will come to us."

"Do that, Ted. Nelson is not stupid, although he sometimes likes to pretend he is."

Nelson was already at the lunch counter but had delayed ordering, knowing that Ted might be late on a Monday. He gave the orders for both of them as Ted came in, and they were soon munching thick sandwiches with liberal dosages of relish, and drinking chocolate malteds.

"Get the baby to bed all right?" asked Nelson.

"Sound asleep," Ted returned.

They ordered cherry pie and Nelson asked:

"What's new on the Grover Hale case?"

Ted frowned. "I'm not exactly sure whether I've come up with anything or not," and he told Nelson about the witnesses he had interviewed.

"Wow!" was his reaction. "It sounds to me like you might as well forget the whole thing, as far as those witnesses are concerned."

"Maybe it isn't quite as bad as it sounds," Ted replied. "Just suppose I found a twenty-dollar bill on my way to work this morning. I might get rather excited about it, and later I might not be able to remember exactly where I found it."

"I would," Nelson retorted. "I'd look around carefully—to make sure nobody saw me."

Ted smiled and resumed, "Here you have ten different people, hurrying about their own business. Suddenly there's the noise of brakes, taking their minds off themselves. Many of the witnesses were not in a good position to see, but somehow they each arrived at their own idea of what was going on. They looked for a little while, and with nothing exciting happening, they soon returned to their own affairs.

"You really couldn't expect them to notice anything *before* the incident. And yet I suppose they tried to decide what had happened just before the accident, and if it seemed logical, they might believe they really saw it. I suppose if we were to question them about that red truck, we'd run into all sorts of opinions on how fast it was going, how long it took it to stop, and so on. You might do the same thing."

"Not me," said Nelson decidedly. "When I don't know something, I'm sure I don't know it. Ask my professors."

"As it happens we're not interested in the truck, though it might help if we knew a little more about that dog. So far none of the witnesses has said he saw the dog getting out of that car."

"Why don't you ask Mr. Dobson?" Nelson suggested. "You told me he saw the dog, too."

Ted looked at Nelson with admiration. "And I thought *I* was supposed to be the reporter around here. I forgot we had a witness in our own office. I don't think it will help too much, though. I wish we could find somebody who noticed the blue car before the accident happened—where it came from, what stores the driver may have stopped at, almost anything at all that would help us."

"Sure," said Nelson cynically, "and if you had ten different witnesses, you'd have ten different stories again."

Ted took out his notebook. "Let's look over these witnesses' stories again and see just what we can get out of them. Now I think that as far as Mrs. Fromand's story goes, we can just forget it. Her story is completely different from all the others. I don't mean that she is lying—I think she saw some other car altogether."

"It might have been the same car at a different time and place," Nelson pointed out.

"Yes, except that she places the time quite close to the time of the accident. Of course she might be wrong about the time, too, but I really can't find anything at all to indicate that the car she saw is the one we want. Now if we compare the other witnesses' stories, there's really not as much difference as you think. They disagree somewhat on the time—the longest difference being about forty minutes—but that's not too bad. One witness had the accident about two blocks away, but that's not so bad, either—and she thought it was a child rather than a dog, but she admits that she didn't get a close look. The men agree pretty well on the make of the car, and the women admit they didn't notice. The description of the car given by some of the women varies, but I think it lies within reasonable bounds, remembering that they weren't much concerned about the blue car anyway. But there's one disturbing fact about the whole thing."

"I know what it is," said Nelson, nodding confidently.

"What?" Ted demanded.

"Don't worry, I'm not going to say it until you do. But it's something that makes the whole incident hit straight home."

"Yes," Ted agreed, shaking his head. "It's that young man seen getting out of the car. They've given various estimates of his age, from about eighteen to thirty, but that's not so bad. Some of the witnesses couldn't have seen him very well, and they must have estimated his age from the way he acted rather than from his appearance.

And they agreed that he was well-dressed, and was seen removing his suitcase from the car."

"Does Ken Kutler know anything about Marty Blaine?"

"No—how could he? I didn't mention to him that I had a visitor Saturday night, and if I had there wouldn't have been any reason to connect him with Grover Hale. As far as I know, Marty simply arrived at the bus terminal, walked over to the newspaper office where I met him and later went home with me."

"He's about the right age, Ted. He arrived just after the accident, and he was well-dressed and carrying a suitcase. Was there anything about Marty to arouse your suspicions?"

"Not at that time, except that his suitcase was rather heavy, but that's nothing. It was none of my business what he was carrying in his suitcase though it seemed to me he was pretty careful that I shouldn't see inside. I know he kept it locked."

"How much does money weigh?" Nelson inquired.

"You're crazy, Nel. That stolen money—or stocks or bonds or whatever it was—couldn't have been in that suitcase. Marty never stole anything from the bank."

"But Hale did—or so they say. He could have passed it on to Marty."

"But why?"

"Because he didn't want to get caught with it himself—natch."

"But Marty said he'd never been inside the Stantonville Bank. He probably didn't even know Hale."

"What do you expect them to do, come right out and say they've been buddies for years?"

"You don't really think Marty is mixed up in this bank embezzlement, do you?"

"No," said Nelson slowly. "We know Marty, and I don't think he's that kind. I mean I can't picture him as a big brain getting involved in a master plot. But he's the kind who sort of stumbles into things without really meaning to. He might find himself involved by feeling he has to protect a friend, or he might have had some personal problems that he just couldn't work out. But I know that if the police knew about Marty, they'd be very anxious to talk with him."

"Yes, I believe you're right, and that may be all the more reason why it's important for us to talk with Marty first. There were several other things that happened after you left, Nel. After we went upstairs, he went down again to make a phone call. He said he was calling for the weather report, but I don't think he was."

"Does he know anybody in Forestdale?"

"Not that I know of. How about long distance?"

"I don't think he'd dare. The call would be on your phone bill at the end of the month. Even if he reversed the charges, there'd be a record of the call."

"There was one more thing," added Ted. "He went downstairs again and outside during the night. I don't know how long he was gone, but I heard him coming back in, and went down myself. There's no doubt he was worrying about something. I think he was on the point of telling me about it, but decided against it."

Nelson began to attack his cherry pie. "Did you find out why they are so sure Grover Hale came to Forestdale?"

"Because he mentioned to a fellow employee that he was driving up here to see a friend."

"All right—if he really embezzled the bank's money, do you think he'd tell anybody where he was going?"

"Maybe, because he said that before he knew the bank examiner was coming in."

"And then, after the bank examiner arrived, he went to the same place anyway? That doesn't sound very logical."

"Put that way, it doesn't. But he may have been rattled, or he may not have had any place else to go. Suppose he had a suitcase to get rid of. He'd have to do his best to keep an appointment he had arranged for that purpose. He may have mentioned his trip to Forestdale just to put an innocent air on the thing. Maybe afterward he forgot he'd mentioned it, or he hoped the other clerk would forget it."

"That's a lot of 'maybes,' " Nelson commented, between bites of pie.

"I suppose it is," Ted agreed.

"The way it looks to me, Ted, this Grover Hale may have come to Forestdale to meet a friend. Marty made a telephone call late at night, and perhaps went out later to meet someone. How do we know that the person Marty met wasn't Grover Hale?"

"Why would he have to meet Hale? If he had received the suitcase from him in the afternoon, I should think they'd try to avoid each other after that."

"But they might have had other details they had to work out, and they wouldn't want to do it over the telephone for fear of being overheard. Well, when do we start after Marty, Ted?"

"Whoa! I'm a working man, remember?"

"Sure you are, and all you've got to do is put the bug in Mr. Dobson's ear and he'll say go to it. You'll ask him, won't you?"

"Sure, I'll ask him. And if you're right, get ready for a long trip."

CHAPTER 6

TED'S HUNCH

TED LOST NO TIME in putting his proposition to Mr. Dobson. He recalled Marty Blaine's arrival at the crucial time, and mentioned the other things that had led him to fear Marty might be involved with Grover Hale. He knew that he could rely on the editor's discretion, for these were things he would not have told the police. When he had finished his account, Mr. Dobson understood the implied question.

"I think, Ted, that the best thing for you to do is to go look for Martin Blaine."

"Thanks, Mr. Dobson," Ted returned, and was unable to hide the eagerness in his voice. "I'll have Nelson drive me, if it's all right with you."

"Excellent, Ted. Don't I see him parked a little way down the street? He's standing around as though undecided whether or not to put a dime into the parking meter."

"That's Nel. Some things he doesn't mind paying, and some things he does."

"Tell him to put it on his expense account. That may make him feel better about it."

"I'll tell him, but I don't think it will. He'll say it's the principle of the thing."

Mr. Dobson smiled, then returned to the matter at hand. "Are you sure you can find Martin, Ted?"

"No, I'm not, Mr. Dobson. All I know is that he said he was leaving for his aunt's farm, forty miles south of Forestdale."

"Well, Ted, one person's forty miles might be another person's thirty miles and still another person's fifty miles. And 'south' could cover quite a wide range on the compass. But do the best you can. Follow it up as long as it seems worth while. If you find you can't get back tomorrow, call in."

"I will," Ted promised. He started to leave, then turned back. "Did you get a good look at that dog Saturday, Mr. Dobson?"

"Yes, I did."

"What color was it?"

"All white."

"You're sure of that? No brown spots?"

"No, Ted, I'm sure. It belongs to the Klause family over on Sterling Avenue. I called Mrs. Klause after you left Saturday. She says she often ties the dog out, but he's learned to slip out of his collar. She's promised to buy him a new one. Is it important?"

"Just checking up on one of my witnesses. See you tomorrow, probably, Mr. Dobson."

"Good hunting, Ted."

Ted arrived at the car just in time to save a reluctant Nelson from inserting a dime in the slot. Technically it was not necessary, since he had not left the car and had stopped only to make a delivery—if Ted could be considered a delivery.

"I don't mind paying for driving on the streets," Nelson complained, "but I hate to pay for not driving on them. Where to, Ted?"

"Drop me off home, and I'll pack a bag. You'll need a bag, too."

"You think we're going to be gone for a week?"

"Who knows?" Ted smiled, and added, "Who cares?"

Ted's bag was quickly packed, and he wrote a hurried note for his mother explaining his absence. Then they stopped at Nelson's where a similar errand was performed. Before two o'clock they were on the road headed south toward Stanton. Or rather, more strictly speaking, the road slanted a little more toward the southwest than they cared to go, and Nelson soon turned off onto a secondary road which led more directly southward.

"But for all we know, Ted, maybe he did mean southwest instead of south. He didn't have any reason to pinpoint it more exactly."

"No, but there's better farmland down this way. Anyway, about the best thing we can do is go directly south for forty miles, and use that as our starting point. We can fan out from there."

"If he really went south, Ted."

"Well, we're starting on the assumption that Marty is innocent, or at worst accidentally blundered into something."

"Sure," Nelson muttered darkly, "like Hitler blundered into a war. All right, suppose we get down to your starting point. What do we do after that?"

"Inquire around. Rural areas aren't like the city. In a large city you may not even know the name of the family next door, but in the country people seem to know everybody for twenty miles around."

"So we ask the first person we meet if he ever heard of Martin Blaine, and he'll say, 'Why, sure, he used to pick strawberries for me ten years ago when he was in knee-pants.' "

Ted pondered carefully. "Well, I don't suppose it will be as easy as all that. The devil of it is that we don't know his aunt's name. I've been wondering if Marty purposely avoided mentioning the name to me, but maybe he didn't. It could have been just an oversight, or simply that he didn't think it mattered. When you come right down to it, we don't even know Marty's home address. I always assumed he lived somewhere near college, because he went home occasionally for weekends, but he never really said."

"Couldn't we telephone the college and get some information about him?"

"They might not want to give it over the phone. And if they did, then we'd have to locate his guardian, and the whole would probably end up in not finding Marty in time to do us any good."

"You mean before the police find him," said Nelson.

"Well, we don't know that the police are even looking for him, but I'd just as soon not give anybody any ideas—including his guardian. No, I can only think of one thing to do. We'll begin by assuming that his aunt has the same last name as he does. We'll inquire for the Blaine farm, and if that doesn't work we'll ask if anybody knows Martin Blaine. I don't suppose anybody would remember him, though. He was just a summer visitor, and a kid at that."

With a map spread out on his knees, Ted carefully measured off forty miles straight south, and Nelson directed the car toward that point, reaching it in the middle of the afternoon.

"I think this is about it, Ted. But it's forty-eight miles on the speedometer. How do you know he didn't mean forty miles driving, instead of a straight line?"

"We don't know. We'll just have to try one thing at a time."

"How is Marty at math, Ted?"

"It's his weak subject, I think. Why?"

"If he was good at figures I'd trust his forty miles. Now I don't know. We aren't even sure we're in the right county, and how many farms do you think there are in a county, anyway?"

"I wouldn't know, but from the way Marty talked I thought it was a small, old-fashioned farm. I don't think his aunt was earning a living on it, by present-day standards. There's a farmer who doesn't look too busy. Let's stop and ask him."

Nelson drew off to the side of the road and parked. They got out of the car and walked over to the fence, and the farmer came over to meet them.

"Eggs, apples, cider?" the farmer questioned. "My son runs a stand. Just turn up that next lane. There's a sign in front."

"Well, no," Ted returned. "We're trying to locate someone. Do you know a Mrs. Blaine? We're looking for the Blaine farm."

The farmer did not seem at all put out. "No, there's no one around here by that name."

"Actually, we're looking for her nephew, a young college student by the name of Martin Blaine. Would you know him?"

"Can't say that I do, but if he ever went to school here, my kids would know. You could ask them."

"No, I don't think he ever went to school here."

"You say that the Blaine farm isn't around here," Nelson broke in. "How far are you sure it isn't?"

"He means how far do we have to go on before we inquire again?" Ted interpreted.

"Well, there's no Blaine farm in this township, that I know. I don't claim to know every farmer in the whole county. But if the Blaines have been around for a long time, I should have heard of them."

"How big is a township?" asked Nelson.

"Six miles by six miles, if it's square."

"Is this one square?"

"Square as your handkerchief," said the farmer solemnly.

They thanked the farmer for his help, but when they returned to the car they were a bit discouraged.

"Where do we go from here, Ted? If the Blaine farm isn't in this township, we have to look in a different one. There's a township on each side of this one, so that makes four more—eight, if you count the ones just touching at the corners."

"Well, the only way to go is north or south, at least till we come to a crossroad," said Ted wryly.

"I think we overshot the mark, Ted. Remember the speedometer said forty-eight miles. Maybe we should have stopped to make inquiries along the way."

"But remember we passed through a long stretch of woods and marginal lands. There wasn't much in the way of farming going on up there. Let's not go back. We'll just follow our noses until something happens."

"If people really followed their noses, something would happen, all right, but it wouldn't be good. What I think, Ted, is that you just hate to turn around. It's like admitting defeat."

"Oh, I'd be willing to go back if I thought our chances were better there. The real thing that's bothering me is the aunt's name. Her farm might be right here after all."

"Blaine might be her maiden name. But if it was, and her family lived around here, or she was married here, I think the farmer would have recognized her name."

"Well, I suppose if you come right down to it, the odds are against her married name being Blaine. But I don't know where else to start. There isn't any local newspaper—I know that, because the *Town Crier* circulates down here. But maybe a court house, or a public library, would be of some help. Let's drive on and see."

They reached a small village five miles farther on, having passed only one crossroad that was narrow, poorly kept and unpromising. They did not know whether they were still in the same township for no signs were posted, and they did not know how close to the edge of the township they had been when they talked to the farmer.

"But it sounded like we were right about in the middle of it from the way he talked," Ted recalled.

"People always sound like they're in the middle. That's where they start measuring from. That does look like a sort of town hall though, Ted. Let's see what they've got there."

They found that the town hall contained some records. But the obliging clerk was unable to find any deeds, marriage licenses or birth certificates under the name of Blaine. They learned by questioning him that they were indeed in a different township, but he was reasonably certain that there had been no family by that name anywhere in the township within recent years. He had never heard of Martin Blaine, and Ted's impression of the aunt as a widow trying to keep up on a run-down farm struck no responsive chord. They expressed their thanks and left.

"Want to go on, Ted? We're forty-five miles south of Forestdale now, and well over fifty miles by driving distance."

"No, there doesn't seem much use going on in this direction, if Marty was anywhere near accurate. Maybe that little old winding road we passed was the right one after all."

Nelson got into the car, and Ted, starting to follow him, suddenly changed his mind. He stood for a few moments leaning against the car, thinking deeply. At last he straightened up.

"I'm going back in there. I thought of another question to ask the clerk."

"What's that?" asked Nelson, getting out to join him.

"Let's inquire about the *Martin* farm."

Nelson looked at him peculiarly. "The heat got you, son? Martin is Marty's *first* name, remember?"

"I know, but let's try it."

They returned to the office, and as soon as Ted mentioned the Martin farm, the clerk's face immediately lighted up.

"Why, of course. You must mean the Reverend Mr. Martin, who died about a year ago. He was very popular around here. And of course Mrs. Martin still lives at the same place and is trying to carry on with the farm—a little place called Meadows. The farm was only a part-time occupation with Mr. Martin, of course, and I suppose Mrs. Martin has a pension to help her out."

Ted's face lit up. "Can you direct us there, please?"

"Surely. It's that crossroad about three miles back. Turn right— that's east—and you'll find it a few miles down the road. I'm sure you can't miss it."

At the car Nelson squinted at Ted.

"I can see your wheels turning, but I still don't know what makes them turn. How'd you ever get an idea like that?"

"I guess you were the one who gave it to me. You said that Blaine might be the aunt's maiden name. That's what started me thinking."

"Let me get this straight. You mean the aunt's maiden name was Blaine?"

"No—or at least I doubt it. Let's begin with Mr. Martin. His sister was Marty's mother. Her maiden name was Martin, and she married a man named Blaine. But I remembered that it's the custom in some families to give the oldest boy the mother's maiden name as his first name. That gives us Martin Blaine. You had the right idea all along, only you didn't know what you had."

"Sure, the way a lot of people discovered penicillin before Fleming, but didn't know it. Anyway, if you had explained this hunch of yours to me ahead of time, I would have said there wasn't one chance in a hundred of your being right."

"I know, but if it's the only idea you've got, why not try it?"

"Well, O.K., Ted, at least we're on the right trail. But we still aren't sure we're going to find Marty at Meadows."

CHAPTER 7

MEADOWS

AS THE CLERK had assured them, they had no trouble finding the Martin farm. The name was lettered plainly on the rural mail box.

"And the way I figure it," Ted pointed out, as they turned into the farmyard, "we're just about forty-two miles from Forestdale, so Marty called it pretty accurately, after all."

A large dog came bouncing out to meet the car, challenging them with all the power of his vocal cords. Then, having performed this duty, he came up to them and allowed himself to be petted, wagging his tail vigorously.

"Some watchdog," Nelson remarked. "He'd lick the hand that stole his bone."

"What's he supposed to do?" Ted retorted. "He alarmed his owner. What more can you expect? It's up to Mrs. Martin to decide whether we're friends or enemies."

"Well, then, where's Mrs. Martin? You don't see her anywhere, do you?"

"No," Ted was obliged to agree.

He looked toward the large, rambling farmhouse with some perplexity. The doors and windows were all closed. It certainly didn't seem that Mrs. Martin was at home. There was nothing particularly strange about that since she might have gone away and left the dog running at large. But the chickens were out in their yard, too, and he thought it likely that they would have been put into their coop if she expected to be gone very long. There was always the possibility of a summer storm, and chickens were not the brightest animals on a farm.

"If Mrs. Martin is here she ought to have heard that barking," Nelson observed. "You don't suppose this is an animal farm, do you, where the animals run everything themselves?"

"I doubt it," said Ted with a grin. "But anyway I imagine Mrs. Martin will be coming home soon. I think I heard a cow in the barn, and cows have to be milked every twelve hours, don't they?"

"Something like that," Nelson answered. He looked around critically. "It looks like this farm could use a little modernizing. I wonder how big it is?"

There was really no way for them even to guess. There was a fairly large kitchen garden back of the house—about as much as a woman would care to handle for her own use, it appeared—and an orchard as well. There were also several acres planted with various grains and behind these, woods could be seen. There was no sign of the activity to be expected on a busy farm on a pleasant day. Perhaps Mrs. Martin really was trying to run everything by herself. If so, she would probably be very glad to have Marty pay her a visit and give her a hand. But where was Marty? If there was an errand to do, why didn't one person tend to it, and the other carry on with the business of running the farm?

"Maybe there just wasn't anything to do," said Nelson lightly, and Ted gave him a severe glance.

"Just try to tell that to any farmer. Usually they're up before sunrise and keep going till dark or after. If I was looking for an easy job, I wouldn't take up farming. Well, I guess you're right about one thing. We still haven't found Marty."

"We haven't looked very hard," Nelson pointed out.

"I know. Let's just say that Marty hasn't found *us*. If he's anywhere within sound of that dog's barking, he's deliberately keeping out of sight. How about looking around?"

He walked closer to the house, and looked it over from several sides.

"What do you think about it?" he asked of Nelson in a low voice, as though afraid of being overheard.

"Think about it? Well, I suppose it would be a nice place to spend a roughing-it type of vacation. But if I were going to live here all year, I think I'd like something a little better than this. It could do with some fixing up."

"How old do you figure it is?"

"Well, it's either a pretty new house that's been allowed to run down, or else it's a pretty old house that's been kept up fairly well."

"I think it's pretty old," was Ted's considered opinion. "Look how some of the boards on the siding don't quite match the others. I don't suppose there would be any harm in trying the door, just to make sure it's locked. After all, a person living all alone might be taken suddenly ill and there would be no one around to help."

He tried both the front and then the rear doors, but they were firmly locked. He shrugged. There seemed no doubt that Mrs. Martin was away, and Marty was gone, too—if he had ever been there. The boys started off toward the barn, looking all about them with great interest as they walked. They passed a pen and a group of small pigs came running out as if they expected to be fed, but the boys had nothing to offer, and went on. The dog was following them closely, as though appreciating the chance for some human companionship, which only added to their belief that they were alone on the farm.

"Maybe he's hungry, too." The thought occurred to Nelson, and he hurried over to the car where they had left a bag of doughnuts purchased on the way. He tossed a doughnut to the dog, who gobbled it up hungrily. It didn't look as though he had been fed for some time. But then you couldn't be sure. Some dogs ate anything.

The dog was looking for more. Nelson hesitated, not because he begrudged the doughnuts, but because he knew that this wasn't exactly customary food for a dog, and Mrs. Martin might object. However, the dog still seemed hungry, and Nelson compromised by breaking another doughnut in half, and throwing one section to the dog. This piece also disappeared.

"I wonder when he was fed last?"

"Probably last night," Ted decided. "I imagine these large farm dogs get fed once a day in the evening. He might be getting hungry by now, even though he hasn't been neglected. Is there something on his collar? It's hard to see, with all that shaggy hair."

Nelson examined the collar more closely. "It looks like 'Condor.' That must be his name. I don't see any license, but maybe you don't need one out here in the country. Here, Condor, here, Condor," he called, and the dog came promptly. "He must be trained."

"Trained to come for doughnuts, anyway," agreed Ted. "Well, let's look in the barn."

"You're sure this is all right, Ted?" asked Nelson cautiously. "I mean, you're always telling me it's illegal to break into somebody's house. How about breaking into somebody's barn?"

"Well, I imagine that's a little bit different, as long as you don't intend any harm. But I wasn't planning on breaking in. If it's locked up, then that's that. But it's just possible that Mrs. Martin has fallen somewhere and needs help. We'll look if we can."

They found that the stable door was not locked, and they walked in. There were three cows inside. They seemed to have enough to eat, and continued munching.

"But shouldn't they be out in the pastures, getting their own food on a nice day like this?" asked Nelson, frowning. "You don't get rich feeding your cows hay in summer."

"I suppose they should. Maybe Mrs. Martin knew she was going to be away for a while. Or maybe this is a supplement to their regular diet. Well, let's go upstairs."

They passed a number of empty stalls on their way to the stairs. It appeared that at one time the farm had been run on a larger basis than it was at the present time. Upstairs, although it was still dim, they could see a little better than they could in the darker part of the stable below. There was hay in the lofts, and a big wagon in the center of the room, with granaries off to the side.

"But I don't know what good that wagon is, without a team of horses to pull it," said Nelson critically.

"Couldn't you pull it with a tractor?"

"Sure, you could pull it with slaves, if you had them. I don't see any signs of a tractor, or any other modern machinery. Another thing is that this wagon looks like it's been sitting here for years without being used. Look how the dust has settled on these hitching poles, and I'll bet it would have been shaken off in quick order, if horses were pulling it. What happened to Condor?"

"He didn't come upstairs with us. He must have run off somewhere."

"How did he get out of the barn? We closed the door, didn't we?"

"Just the lower half. Maybe he could leap over it. Or maybe he can manipulate the latch. Let's look out and see."

The boys moved to the end of the room and threw open an upper section of a door. They could now look down upon a haystack not far below them in an enclosed barnyard. They heard a bark, and spotted Condor off in the distance, apparently on the track of something. Whether he had scared up a rabbit or some other animal, they could not tell, but he seemed to know what he was doing. The sun was setting and the fine summer day was drawing to a close.

They closed the door, went downstairs—found the lower door still latched—and stepped outside again. There they had a brief discussion on what to do. They were growing hungry. And what should they do about Mrs. Martin—and Marty?

"Look, Ted," said Nelson, "I don't know about this any more. You think Mrs. Martin ought to be coming home soon, but it's going to be dark before we know it. We haven't found her, and as long as we haven't found her I'm not sure we have any business here. And if she isn't here, and we want to find her, we ought to be looking somewhere else. At the same time, I can't help but feel that she might need our help around here. What's going to happen to all these animals if we desert them? I don't know much about farming, but these cows are supposed to be milked every twelve hours."

"I wonder if it matters much if you're a little late? Surely someone ought to be around here before long."

"I remember that my uncle was pretty strict about getting his cows milked right on time."

"What time did your uncle milk?"

"I don't know about morning—usually I wasn't up. In the evening he milked right after supper—around seven o'clock, I suppose. But maybe he did that because it fitted in with the milk collection schedules. I suppose it doesn't matter when you decide to milk your cows, as long as you stick to your schedule."

"But we don't know that these cows are on a seven o'clock schedule."

"No, but I don't think it could be much later than that or it would make the chores pretty late in the morning."

"Maybe Mrs. Martin doesn't have to worry about collection schedules if she doesn't try to sell her milk."

"Well, if she uses it all herself she must have plenty, so I'm sure she wouldn't mind if we took a little for ourselves."

Then Ted suddenly got the idea. "You mean *you're* going to try to milk a cow? You're a town boy, remember?"

"I know, but I remember how my uncle used to do it, and it didn't look very hard. You dare me?"

"No dares," Ted decided. "It's still early. Let's look the farm over a little more. Then when we get back we can give your idea another whirl."

"O.K., but don't wait till dark. I won't milk any cow in the dark."

They set off on a short tour of the farm, which took them beyond the fields and up to the very edges of the woods. Everything seemed to be in reasonably good shape. The fences were in repair, the kitchen garden was weeded, the fruit trees were coming along nicely. Somewhere along their walk, Condor came racing up to them, panting excitedly.

"Where've you been, boy?" asked Nelson leaning over to pet him, but he didn't get much of an answer. The dog was satisfied to trot along quietly beside them.

As they returned to the drive where their car was parked, Nelson noticed something.

"Say, that shed there. Isn't that a car in there?"

He hurried over to the shed, with Ted close at his heels. The door was latched but not locked. Opening it, they saw that Nelson had indeed been right. It was a car of not-too-recent vintage. They walked all around the car, and discovered that a front fender had been badly damaged, although it probably did not scrape the wheel.

"I wonder when that happened?" said Nelson thoughtfully.

"What difference does it make? It might have been months ago."

"I don't think so, Ted. See these little flakes of paint? They would all have fallen off by this time, if it happened very long ago."

"Unless the car wasn't used."

"But it *has* to be used, Ted. What do you think farmers are? They have to get around. If you don't have a horse, a car is your only means of keeping in touch with the world. There aren't any busses or trolleys out here, and most places are too far away to walk. And what about all the hauling you have to do?"

"She might have two cars, Nel. This is a passenger car. She might have had a kind of pick-up truck, too, or at least a station wagon."

"Not if she is as hard up as you've been trying to make me believe. On the small scale she's been operating, I imagine she'd be able to get by with this car. Besides, it's just the right age."

"What do you mean?"

"It's not too new, and it's not too old. If she had a new car, she might not want to use it for rough stuff. And if this was an old car it might not be dependable enough, and she'd save it only for emergencies. But I'll bet you this is probably her only car. She uses it all the time."

"Except today," Ted amended. "I wonder where she would have gone without her car? I don't even see any neighbors close by she might have walked over to visit."

"She could have gone somewhere in somebody else's car, Ted. Well, it's getting darker. If I'm going to milk that cow, I'm not waiting any longer."

CHAPTER 8

HOW TO MILK A COW

THERE WERE electric wires stretched to the barn, and after a little trouble they found a light switch. But when they pressed it nothing happened. They traced the wires back toward a small shed housing a generator, but since they did not know how to start the generator and did not want to take the responsibility of tampering with it, they were no better off than they were before.

"Looks like I'll have to milk the cows by flashlight," Nelson decided.

"You're sure you know how to do this?" Ted questioned doubtfully.

"Look, milking a cow is something any ten-year-old farm boy can do."

"Unless machinery has spoiled him."

"Don't worry about that. Farm boys still have to know how to milk cows. What if the current is off, or the milking machines break down?"

"Well, all right. How do you begin?"

Nelson surveyed the situation with his flashlight. There was a small stool by the cow stalls, and he had already picked up a clean milk bucket. For the first time he seemed uncertain.

"Now I know you're always supposed to milk from a certain side, but I forget which side it is."

"How about the left side?" Ted suggested.

"No, I think that's the side you mount a horse on. I guess I'll try the right side. There seems to be a little more room there."

"Watch out you don't get kicked," Ted warned him.

"Oh, I'll be careful. My uncle always said if you've got a horse that kicks frontward or backward, you can train him, but if you've got a horse that kicks sideways, get rid of him."

"Only these are cows," Ted pointed out.

But try as Nelson would, he was unable to start a flow of milk into the pail. Doggedly, he continued, determined to make a success of his project if he possibly could, but at last the cow began to show a certain impatience.

"The heck with it," he decided. "Maybe this one's dry. I'll try the next one."

But he was no more successful with either the second cow or the third. At last he was obliged to admit defeat.

"I guess that settles it," he said. "I'm never going to be a farmer—or even a farm boy. It's a good thing for us there's a country store near here where we can buy all the milk we want—and cold, too."

"That seems like carrying atoms to Oak Ridge," said Ted with a smile. "I'm not too hungry, though. I won't have any trouble getting by till morning. I wonder where we're going to sleep?"

"I guess we'll have to hit the hay—and I mean that just the way it sounds."

But Ted was still concerned about the animals.

"It seems to me they ought to be fed, and maybe we ought to get the pigs and chickens back inside. Condor must be hungry, too. I wonder just what is going on around here."

The boys stepped outside the barn and suddenly Condor began his loud barking again. A car had turned into the drive.

"At last," said Nelson in relief, but he spoke too soon. For when the driver had parked the car and got out they saw that it was neither Mrs. Martin nor Marty, but a stranger. He came directly toward them, and gave them a friendly but questioning greeting.

"You boys friends of Mrs. Martin?"

"Not exactly," Ted replied. "I'm Ted Wilford, from the Forestdale *Town Crier*, and this is my friend, Nelson Morgan."

"And I'm Emil Pierson. I have the next farm, down the road a piece. Are you looking for Mrs. Martin?"

"Either for her or her nephew, Martin Blaine. Do you know him?"

"Why, of course I know him. He used to pal around with my son when he was here on vacations. I understood he was staying here now. I make it a point to have some member of my family stop by here every day to see if Mrs. Martin needs some help. My son usually does the heaviest work on the farm, but Mrs. Martin is a strong, independent woman, and won't let him do anything she can do for herself. I didn't stop today because I thought Marty was here and I wouldn't be needed. Then I noticed there were no lights on in the house and thought it was a little too early for that, so I decided to look in. Where is Mrs. Martin?"

"We thought maybe you could tell us that," Ted returned.

"No, I'm afraid I don't have any idea," said the farmer, shaking his head. "It isn't like her to be away like this. The evening chores need tending to. Whenever she's been unavoidably absent, she's always left word with my Harve so he could come over and tend to things. But this time she didn't call."

"When is the last time you saw her?" asked Nelson, speaking for the first time.

"Yesterday morning at church. She told me then about going to pick up her nephew at the bus stop."

"Where is this bus stop?"

"Out on the main road—where this road joins Route 57. It won't do any good to go there, though. It's just a signpost stuck in the ground. Nothing else there except a service station, and that's closed on Sunday."

"What about these animals?" asked Ted, indicating the chickens nearby.

"They'll have to be tended to, of course. Better leave that to me, since I know how things are supposed to be handled. You're a newspaperman. Think you can do anything about finding Mrs. Martin?"

"I can certainly try. In fact, we'll start right now if there's nothing we can do here."

"No, I can handle it. I've got my own chores at home, but Harve will take care of them if I'm not there."

"Would you mind if I watched you milk a cow?" asked Nelson. "I tried it a little while ago, but I couldn't get the hang of it."

"Well, it takes a little knack, but my Harve was able to milk by the time he was seven years, eight months. Course he was big for his age. Milking is hard work, and don't let anybody tell you different. That's why milking machines were invented."

They entered the barn together. The farmer snapped the light switch, but once again it failed to respond.

"Generator must be off. I could get it running for you if you need-ed it, but I can get along without it myself."

"Then don't bother for us. We'll be leaving in a minute."

Mr. Pierson sat down on the milking stool by the light of a lantern and set about his task. But surprisingly enough, he had no better luck than Nelson, getting only the merest trickle.

"What do you know?" he said in surprise. "This cow's been milked already."

"What!" the boys exclaimed together.

"Sure as you're born. I'll try the others, just to make sure."

He did, and had no better luck.

"This isn't a joke, is it? You boys didn't milk the cows, did you?"

"I should say not," Nelson retorted. "I mean I tried, but I couldn't. And Ted was laughing himself silly! Well, I don't think the joke is on me any more."

"No," the farmer agreed, "but I'm not sure just who is the goat. Well, I'll tend to the rest of the things. If you boys find out anything about Mrs. Martin, give me a ring tonight, will you? That'll help me plan my work for tomorrow, because somebody'll have to take care of things here."

"We'll do that," Ted pledged. "May I have your number?"

"You don't have to bother. Just ring exchange, and ask for me. We have rural service here."

"Oh, Mr. Pierson . . ." Nelson turned back as they were about to get into his car. "Does Mrs. Martin have more than one car?"

"No, just the one. It's in the shed, isn't it? She usually leaves the doors open when she takes it out."

Nelson maneuvered the car around, and they were soon out on the road.

"What do you make of all this, Ted?" he asked.

"Well—Mrs. Martin has certainly disappeared somehow."

"But her car came back," Nelson pointed out. "I could under-stand if she disappeared with her car, but this way . . ."

Ted thought it over carefully. "As far as we know, everything must have been all right until she left to go to meet Marty's bus. Then something must have happened. Maybe she had an accident along the way. Or maybe she met Marty, and then something he told her led her to go off somewhere."

"With all the stock left alone like that, and without calling Mr. Pierson? That doesn't sound like her. She'd know the neighbors would be worrying."

"Maybe not, not if . . ."

"If what?" Nelson demanded, as Ted paused.

"Well, look at it like this. We know her car came back. We know the cows were milked. When do you think they were milked?"

"Why—I thought maybe before we came."

"Well, think again. We've been hanging around Meadows for hours. If they had been milked that long ago I'm pretty sure there would have been more milk than we got, and Mr. Pierson wouldn't have said the cows had been milked; he would have said somebody must have milked them that afternoon. So the cows must have been milked while we were taking our little walk around the farm. Somebody must have been keeping an eye on us all the time. He wouldn't have milked ahead of time, because he wouldn't have known we were coming. But he knew the cows had to be milked, and managed it at just about the right time. The rest of the stock wasn't neglected, either. He would have made sure everything was done up for the night."

"But who . . ." Nelson asked, and as Ted did not respond immediately, he thought about it for a moment, then finally whistled. "Marty?"

"Who else?"

Then Nelson laughed. "Well, what do you know about that? Everything seems so mysterious until you think of the right thing, and then it all falls into place. Of course Marty didn't want to see us. I don't think I would want to see anybody either, if I was carrying a suitcase full of umpty-thousand dollars in stolen funds!"

"I thought we agreed Marty didn't have anything to do with that," Ted reminded him.

"That's not what I said, Ted. I said I was sure Marty didn't have anything to do with stealing the money. But he's just the kind of guy who'll be standing on a corner when somebody comes along and asks him please to hold his coat. Then the fellow disappears and Marty finds the crown jewels in the pocket. I'll bet it was something like that. This Grover Hale put the money in the suitcase. He probably gave Marty a lift from the bus station, and then made up some plausible story and Marty offered to take care of the suitcase for him. They met that night and Marty returned the suitcase to him . . ."

"He didn't return it to him," Ted observed. "He still had the suitcase the next day, and it was still heavy."

"I don't mean he returned the suitcase—I mean he returned what was in it."

"But then he must have known what was in it, and I don't think he did. If things happened as you suggest, I still can't believe Marty knew about the money."

"He *must* have known by the middle of the night," Nelson pointed out. "That would be after he heard the police broadcast about the robbery. He couldn't have been so naïve that it didn't put a bug in his bonnet. Now mind you, I think Marty is perfectly honest. But he'd be a sucker for a hard-luck story, and these con men have a wonderful gift of gab. If Marty thought Hale were really innocent, he might have agreed to help him out."

"He couldn't have thought Hale was innocent if he knew Hale had the money."

"Who knows? Hale could pretend it was money that was rightfully due him, or something of the sort."

"Listen, Nel, Marty's a college man remember? And he didn't get there by being a moron."

"No, but he could still be naïve. Now look, Ted. We've got plenty of witnesses who saw Marty getting out of that car driven by Grover Hale. He had a heavy suitcase, and at first he didn't even want you to lift it. But at least he made certain that you never saw what was inside. Am I right so far?"

"I guess so," Ted agreed slowly.

"Now I'll put it up to you. You didn't see the inside of that suitcase. But did you see anything that could have been in it? Did you see Marty in his pajamas, or did he change to a different suit the next day?"

"No, I guess not. But I wouldn't expect him to carry a spare suit around in that little bag. As for his shirt and things, I didn't notice."

"Just the same, it's possible that the suitcase never contained any of his personal things at all. I can't imagine him traveling around without his own suitcase, but maybe it was exchanged in the car, or at least his own things were taken out and replaced with this—this loot."

Then that night he met Grover Hale, and the money was given back to Hale. Either Marty's own things were returned to him, or there was a duplicate suitcase, or maybe they just filled it up with stones to make it as heavy as it was before. How about this, boy?"

Ted thought it over. "If your explanation is true, then Marty is either very guilty or very simple. But suppose for the moment this is true, there are still a few other things to explain. Most important, where is Mrs. Martin?"

"She probably got on the bus. What else would you do at a bus stop? Then Marty brought the car back to the farm."

"But if we look at it this way," Ted argued, "then Mrs. Martin is probably as guilty or as simple-minded as Marty. No, I don't think she would have had anything to do with something like this. There must be another explanation. And as for that wrecked fender on her car, I'm wondering if an accident isn't the answer."

"This is the country, Ted. Any kind of a serious accident, and the news would be all over in jig time. I'm sure Mr. Pierson would have heard about it."

"Maybe not—maybe there were certain reasons why he wouldn't have. Anyway let's try it that way, and see what happens."

"What about Marty? Why don't we root him out of that barn, or wherever he's hiding, and ask him?"

"Because we're not sure yet just what he's been up to, and as a newspaperman I have to play it on the right side. We'll try to see what we can find out for ourselves."

CHAPTER 9

A GAME OF HIDE-AND-SEEK

THE SERVICE STATION was open, and the attendant there said he knew Mrs. Martin very well. But of course, since he had been closed the previous day, he had not seen her waiting at the bus stop.

"Her car seemed to be damaged. Do you think there's any chance she might have been in an accident before she reached the bus stop?" Ted inquired.

"An accident? Well, now, I would have heard if there'd been an accident. I should think she would have brought the car to me for repairs. I can handle most of that kind of work."

"Just a crumpled fender," Nelson put in.

"Well, then, she might not have bothered coming to me. Some people are fussy about the slightest scratch to their cars, and other people don't care, as long as they can get where they want to go. I don't think Mrs. Martin would have cared. She would have been more concerned about the money, since she has to watch her expenses."

"Then you don't know where we can find Mrs. Martin?" asked Ted.

"If she's not on her farm, I wouldn't know where she is. There are some accidents where the car is hardly damaged at all but the occupant is injured. Still, you say the car got back to her farm all right. That doesn't sound like much of an accident."

"Supposing there had been an accident, how would we find out about it?"

"Try the constable. He's about a mile down that way—there's a flag pole in front of his house. He's off duty now, and you can probably reach him there."

Thanking the attendant, the boys were soon on their way again. They found the house without any difficulty, and were also lucky in finding the constable at home. He listened to their story carefully.

"No, there was no accident reported to me. But I'll admit we don't have the best roads in the world out this way, and there was a heavy rain here Saturday night. The driving would have been none too good on Sunday. Maybe Mrs. Martin did have some sort of trouble while driving to the bus stop Sunday afternoon."

"If she did, where would she have gone?" asked Ted anxiously, while Nelson, too, hung on the constable's answer.

"Apparently she wasn't so badly hurt that she was unable to drive, and the car must have been in operating condition, too. The most likely thing would be our first-aid station in the village hall. But she didn't go there, or I would have heard about it. But if it was serious, the closest place would be the Haverford clinic. They might be able to handle her there."

This was the best lead the boys had, and they decided to follow it up. Having inquired the way to Haverford, they thanked the constable and took their leave.

Haverford turned out to be a very small community, and the clinic consisted of three doctors practicing as a group. But they had no hospital facilities, and bed patients were transferred to the large hospital in Centerage.

The nurse at the desk assured them that no Mrs. Martin had been treated at the clinic during the last day or two. Of course it was possible that she had gone directly to Centerage, without being referred there by the clinic.

Centerage was some distance away, and it would be ten o'clock before the boys could get there. Still, everything considered, they decided they had better go on with it. Even if they were unable to talk with Mrs. Martin, just knowing whether or not she was there would make their problems a little easier. They had promised to call Mr. Pierson that night, and it would be better if they had something definite to tell him. So far they had no proof that Mrs. Martin had been injured, or even that Marty had ever arrived at Meadows.

The receptionist at the hospital desk cleared up one piece of the puzzle.

"Yes," she answered Ted's question about Mrs. Martin, "Mrs. Karen Martin was admitted here last evening, following an auto accident. Her condition is good."

Ted and Nelson exchanged glances; apparently Ted's hunch had paid off once again.

"Is it possible for us to see her?" Ted requested.

"It's after visiting hours. Is it an emergency?"

Ted wanted to be truthful.

"I'm not exactly certain," he said hesitantly. "We're friends of her nephew. It's just possible that we can relieve her mind on certain matters concerning the farm. On the other hand, we don't want to bother her and if necessary we can come back tomorrow."

The receptionist rose at once. "You'd better come with me now to see her. I know she's been worried over the fact that her nephew failed to visit her this evening, as she had expected. Talking to you may mean the difference between a good night's sleep and a restless one, and that's always important with a patient."

She led the way, and following at a short distance, Ted whispered to Nelson:

"Now remember, we're not supposed to upset her about Marty. As far as we know, he's out there on the farm and we just happened to miss him."

"Anyway we know why he didn't come to visit his aunt. He couldn't, because we were there and we would have seen him leave in the car."

The nurse asked them to wait in the hall while she went in and spoke to Mrs. Martin. Shortly afterward she motioned them in. Mrs. Martin seemed glad to see them.

"Well, I feel as if I've known you boys for a long time. Marty mentioned you occasionally in his letters, and of course I knew he was going to stop off in Forestdale to pay you a visit, Ted, before coming here."

"How did the accident happen?" Ted inquired.

"Oh . . ." She looked puzzled. "I ran my car off the road in all that mud and bumped into a post. Didn't Marty tell you about it?"

"We haven't seen Marty yet," said Ted as smoothly as possible. "We must have missed him at the farm. He wasn't there when we stopped by. We checked with the constable, and that eventually led us here."

"But were the cows milked?" she asked anxiously.

"Oh, yes, Mr. Pierson dropped in while we were there, and he assured us that Marty had milked the cows."

"Oh, well, then, I guess everything must have been all right. I was wondering why Marty didn't come here tonight, but he must have had some affairs of his own to attend to. Or maybe the chores took him longer than he expected, and he found it was too late to come."

"Are you getting along all right, Mrs. Martin?" Ted questioned.

"Oh my, yes. I should have been out of here today. Ordinarily they would simply have kept me overnight for observation, and let me go today. But there is a certain complication. You see, I broke my shoulder rather badly several years ago, and that break still shows up on the X rays. They want to be sure it's the old break, and not something new."

"Can't they tell an old break from a fresh one on the X rays?"

"I suppose they can ordinarily, but this seems to be a special case. When Marty arrived at the bus stop and learned I'd hurt my shoulder again, he insisted on driving me into Centerage where I'd been treated before. But I'm sure there's nothing seriously wrong, and that I'll be going home tomorrow. You tell Marty that, will you?"

"Yes, we will," Ted promised.

"Oh, dear, I just assumed you were going back to Meadows. I don't want you to make a special trip, if that's not what you planned to do. But you did come to see Marty, didn't you?"

"Yes, we did, Mrs. Martin."

"Then I suppose it must have been about something important, or you wouldn't have driven down here all this way."

"Mostly we wanted a little vacation on a farm for a few days," said Nelson. "We're mixing business and pleasure."

"Well, then, you boys must feel free to stay there on the farm just as long as you please. I have an extra key, and I'll ask the nurse to give it to you, just in case you happen to miss Marty again."

"But you don't know us from Adam," Ted objected.

"Nonsense, Ted. You couldn't have spoken about Marty the way you did, unless you were a good friend of his."

Her manner was very assured, and Ted felt a little self-conscious. He knew that he had not tried to explain their reason for wanting to see Marty again, so soon after his visit to Forestdale. It was hard to know what to say since he didn't want to worry her.

"Mrs. Martin, I don't want to make a mystery out of our errand. The fact is that I'm down here on a newspaper story, and it's just possible that Marty can help me. I'm trying to locate a certain man who was seen in Forestdale on Saturday afternoon. I have reason to believe that Marty spoke to him for a few minutes on Saturday, and he may be able to give me some clue as to where this man was going."

"Oh, well, I suppose it's newspaper business that I don't know anything about. But that's all right. I'm sure that Marty wouldn't be mixed up in anything bad. He's a good boy."

She spoke as confidently as before, but Ted felt that her loyalty to Marty was such that she would have considered him a good boy no matter what he had done. While Ted's faith in Marty was as high as ever, he considered it possible that Marty might have blundered into some extraordinary situation.

When the boys rose to go, Mrs. Martin called a nurse who gave them the key to the house. They thanked her, and left, after promising once more to carry her message to Marty.

"Now where, Ted?"

"There's a pay station in the lobby. I want to call Mr. Pierson."

"And tell him what?"

"That Mrs. Martin is in the hospital but not badly hurt, and that Marty is out there on the farm taking care of things, so it won't be necessary for him to worry about it. I have an idea it will be just as well to keep Mr. Pierson out of our way for the next day or two. We'll have trouble enough dealing with Marty."

"But are you even sure Marty's there, Ted?"

"He must be. We know that he arrived on the bus, that he took the car back to the farm and that the cows were milked. I don't think he would take off again, with the stock there to be attended to."

"Not unless we've given him a good fright, Ted. And we have at that. Suppose he took the money here to a quiet farm where he thought he could hide out, and then suddenly he finds we're on his trail. He might just want to get out of there fast."

"If he had the money," said Ted mildly.

"Well, your hunch turned out right about Mrs. Martin's name, and you were right about finding her in a hospital. Why can't one of my hunches turn out right for a change?"

"I don't know that there's any law against it," answered Ted.

"One thing about it, though, Ted. Whatever Marty's up to, I'm pretty sure Mrs. Martin doesn't know anything about it."

"Yes, I imagine you're right about that. But there is something about Marty that worries me. Apparently it was less important to him to visit his aunt tonight than to avoid us. That might be a tough nut to crack—I mean, after we are through playing hide-and-seek with him."

"What's the best way for us to find Marty, Ted?"

"Oh, I don't think we'll have much trouble. How long can you stay hidden on a farm as long as you have certain chores to do? I think Marty was just hoping that we'd give up and leave, when we didn't find him there right away. When he discovers that we've come back and settled down in the house, he'll have to think of some other way to play it."

"Then we aren't going to hunt for him tonight?"

"I'm not. As far as I'm concerned the game's over. I've put in a full day and I'm going to hit the feathers and let Marty hit the hay, as you expressed it. I think we can catch him the first thing in the morning, when it's time to milk the cows."

"Maybe—but what if he decides not to milk the cows?"

"Then I guess you'll have to do it."

"Not me," said Nelson decidedly. He had had his fill of milking by this time. Without actually doing it he had managed to convince both Ted and Mr. Pierson that he could milk a cow, and he was willing to rest on his laurels. "We'll rout Marty out and make him do it. You know, Condor ought to be able to find him. It would be pretty hard to hide from a dog."

"I imagine Condor knew where he was all the time. It must have been Marty who let Condor out of the barn."

Then Ted went to make his call.

CHAPTER 10

A WRESTLING MATCH

THE FARM was still dark when they arrived. Only Condor took some notice of their arrival, and unable to coax another doughnut out of Nelson, soon went peacefully back to sleep. They entered the house and tried to turn on the lights, with the usual result. But Nelson's flashlight was still holding up and they decided to get along with that rather than scout around for candles or lanterns.

They had stopped for something to eat along the way, and had brought some additional supplies with them. Nelson was about to place some of the perishables in the refrigerator, but Ted stopped him.

"Don't open the door. The current is off, and whatever's in there will keep better if you leave the door closed."

Nelson looked around, and spotted a large home freezer. "Well, I hope the power gets back on before *that* starts to thaw out. It could hold Mrs. Martin's whole winter food supply. How long can you go without power before you're in trouble?"

"About twenty-four hours, I think, if you keep it closed."

"Then, we'd better see about getting some current here tomorrow."

"That won't be any problem, if we can find Marty. He probably knows just what to do."

"If we don't find him I think I'll tackle it myself. Anybody who can repair a car ought to be able to figure that thing out. It's the same kind of engine. I wonder how often they do keep the current on around here? Maybe a few hours in the morning and evening is all they need—pump and heat the water, keep the refrigerator and freezer cold, use the household electrical appliances. Then they'd want some light in the evening."

"That's an electric stove, isn't it? It would be hard cooking without that."

"Gee whiz, you do get more dependent on electricity than you realize, don't you? It must be awkward not having current anytime you want it. Maybe she couldn't afford to tap on to the main line. No wonder . . ."

If he was going to make some reference to the bank robbery, Ted's finger to his lips effectively silenced him.

"Let's be careful what we say," said Ted in a whisper. "We don't know where Marty's hiding."

"Want to search the house?"

"It wouldn't hurt to give it a quick going-over. I don't believe there's a basement, is there?"

"I don't see any way to get there from here. It must be just a dug-out for storing vegetables, and you reach it from those doors outside. Anyway, I'm sure she hasn't got a furnace, or she wouldn't be using these old coal stoves for heating. Br-r-r. It makes me cold to think of winter around here."

"You've been spoiled by civilization," Ted scoffed.

The house was long and rambling, but their search of the ground floor did not take long. Then they started up the stairs. They had brought their suitcases from the car, and were prepared to settle down for the night.

"Which bedroom do we take?" Nelson inquired.

"Not this one," said Ted, stopping at the first door. "This looks like Mrs. Martin's bedroom, and I wouldn't want to interfere. And this one," he paused at the next door, "looks like Marty's. What do you think?"

They stepped into the room, and looked around. Some small, masculine effects were out on the dresser. They looked into the closet and found some clothes about Martin's size. Then Nelson suddenly stooped and looked under the bed.

"Hey, Ted!" he called in an excited whisper.

"What's up?" Ted stooped beside him, and saw a suitcase like the one Marty had had in Forestdale.

"That settles it," Nelson decided. "Marty *was* here—we know that for sure, even if he may be gone by now. Let's look around *for sure*, Ted."

Nelson hurried back to look at Mrs. Martin's bedroom once more, while Ted went on to the third bedroom. A quick search there, and in the bathroom and remaining closets, convinced both boys that Marty was nowhere on that floor, and probably not in the house at all. There appeared to be no attic, or at least no stairway to reach it, nor were they successful in finding a trap door anywhere in the ceiling.

"Let's go to bed," Ted decided, sitting down on the bed and beginning to take off his shoes. "We'll have problems enough to keep us busy in the morning."

"We've got problems enough right now," said Nelson determinedly, refusing to follow his example.

"Like what?" asked Ted with a yawn.

"Like that suitcase. Do you realize, Ted, that we might be sleeping here under the same roof with the proceeds from a bank robbery while all the police in the state are on the alert for it? How's that going to sound if you ever have to stand up in court and tell about what we did tonight?"

"Look, you don't know that there's anything valuable in that suitcase, do you?"

"No, but I can imagine. Ted, is there any reason under the sun why I can't go in that bedroom and see what's in that suitcase?"

"None but your conscience. We're here by right of someone's generous hospitality—and that suitcase isn't ours. Now if you want to look into it, go right ahead."

"Well, if you think it's wrong, why don't you try to stop me?"

"You're heavier than I am."

"You could at least try to argue me out of it."

"I did. Now that's all I've got to say about it. You've got to wrestle the thing out with your own conscience."

"Look, Ted, I don't want to abuse hospitality, and I don't want to pry into anyone's personal business. But if Marty really is mixed up in this bank business, it isn't personal any more. If I find out it *is* something from the bank, then I've done my duty, and if I find out it isn't, then whom have I hurt?"

"No one, I suppose. But suppose you did find money or stocks in there, what would you do with them?"

"Why—I don't know."

"I don't know either, and until I figure that out, I'd just as soon not know what's in there."

Nelson thought it over. "The proper thing would be to turn it over to the police, wouldn't it?"

"How could you prove that it came from the bank?"

"Well, hang it, I don't have to draw anybody a blueprint, do I? Anyway, it wouldn't be up to me to prove it."

"All right, suppose for the moment the stuff did come from the bank. If Marty really were in on this thing, you don't think he's in on it alone, do you? Somebody would be watching us, probably somebody with a gun who is prepared to use it. How far do you want to go in starting something?"

"Gosh—I didn't think of that. You still don't believe it's got anything to do with the bank, do you?"

"No, the whole thing looks too casual to me. The suitcase was pushed under the bed where anybody might find it. Marty's clothes are hanging in the closet. I can't see that anybody's trying to hide anything from us."

"Well, if you're right about that, at least there isn't any reason why I can't lift the suitcase, is there? I can see if it's still heavy, the way you said."

"No, I don't suppose anybody can complain about your lifting it," Ted agreed.

Nelson hurriedly left the room, and returned almost at once. "You're right, Ted," he said excitedly. "It *is* heavy, a lot heavier than you'd expect a suitcase that size to be. Whatever was in it then is still in it."

"Or something else that's just about as heavy," Ted responded.

Nelson got into his pajamas, but still wasn't satisfied. "Ted—I don't say I'm going to break into that suitcase, but there wouldn't be any harm in just finding out whether it's locked or not, would there?"

"You go just as far as your conscience lets you," was the only advice Ted would give him.

Faced with this lack of encouragement, Nelson hesitated, but finally made up his mind. He left the room again, and this time was gone a little longer than before. He came back looking discouraged.

"It's locked—locked up tight. I can see why somebody would keep his suitcase locked while he's traveling, but why would he keep it locked in his house—unless it had something very valuable inside? Ted, what's the law about breaking into somebody's locked suitcase?"

"Oh, I imagine it's some sort of felony, but I haven't been to law school."

"Well, the way it looks to me, I might be in trouble with the law if I don't break in, and I might be in trouble with the law if I do break in. What am I supposed to do about that?"

"Get yourself a good lawyer, I suppose."

Reluctantly Nelson got into bed. "All right, Ted, I'll let it go. But you may be sorry. Remember, if Marty shows up tomorrow, our chances of getting into that suitcase may go glimmering."

"Go to sleep," Ted advised him.

"Fat chance," his friend replied. But in spite of his protestations, he was soon asleep, while Ted lay awake for some time longer. In his mind he reviewed the events of the last couple of days, trying to see if there was any explanation or clue which he had so far overlooked. But nothing occurred to him, and at last he, too, fell asleep.

He was awakened some hours later by Nelson, shaking his shoulder urgently. At the same time he held a hand over his mouth so that Ted would make no noise. He had not turned on the flashlight, and the room was nearly pitch black except for the outline of the windowshade.

Arousing himself, Ted pushed Nelson's hand away, and whispered, "What's up?"

"Just listen. Do you hear anything?"

Ted listened as carefully as he could. There did seem to be a faint rustling somewhere in the house, but he wasn't sure. The country is so full of strange noises anyway. It might have been nothing more than the sound of birds on the roof.

"What do you think it is?" he asked.

"You can't hear it so well now. But a while ago it was plainer. I could tell there was somebody coming up the steps. Someone else is in this house now, Ted."

"Probably Marty. Maybe he got tired of sleeping out in the barn. He's probably ready to tell us all about it in the morning."

"Want to go and look?"

"No, let's not. Let's give him plenty of rope. The more things he does, the harder it will be for him to explain—except to tell the truth."

"Listen."

This time Ted, too, could hear the quite distinct sound of foot-steps. It seemed that someone was now descending the steps. They listened, breathlessly, until the footfalls ceased. Then Nelson said:

"There may be the suitcase, marching right out of the house and out of our lives. I don't like this sitting here doing nothing, Ted. It seems kind of cowardly to me."

"I've got no objection to being brave, as long as you know what you're being brave about. But that's either Marty, or it's someone else, and if it's someone else, he's probably got a gun. Would you care to argue with that?"

Just then Condor began to bark excitedly.

"He's spotted someone," said Nelson, getting up quietly and peeking past the windowshade. "Now he's quieting down again. Whoever it was seems to have disappeared. Come on, Ted."

"Where to?"

They had not brought robes and slippers with them, but they put on their shoes.

"Here, first," said Nelson, dashing into Marty's room. He looked under the bed. "The suitcase is still here," he said, with some relief. "Well, come on. Let's look at the doors."

They hurried downstairs by the light of Nelson's flashlight. They examined first the front door, and then the back, but neither lock ap-peared to have been tampered with.

"Probably it was Marty," Ted decided, but Nelson only grunted.

He opened the door, and they stepped outside into the dim moon-light. They found that there had been some more rain while they slept, but it had stopped now and the sky was clearing. Condor came running up to them, wagging his tail, and they stopped to pet him. He had done his duty by arousing them, and it was proper to show their appreciation. But the dog still seemed a little suspicious as he cast occasional glances toward the east. It was probably nothing that he saw now, but something he remembered he *had* seen there.

"Does that do it, or do you want to go on?" Ted inquired.

"Oh, I suppose there isn't anything more we can do. We know the suitcase is still there, and if anything else was taken we wouldn't be able to tell about that, anyway. Let's go back in, but let's keep Condor inside with us. I don't like the idea of anybody's trying to break into the house again. Maybe he didn't get what he wanted and has ideas about coming back."

In the kitchen they gave the dog a little snack as a reward, and he gobbled it down, though not exactly ravenously. There could be little doubt that he had been fed at some time since they left the farm. Probably Mr. Pierson had attended to it, although it might have been Marty, too.

"Ted," said Nelson, as they mounted the stairs, while Condor stayed looking after them. He appeared either to be frightened of the stairs, or else had been trained not to go up them, for he made no attempt to follow.

"What?"

"You agree that there *was* somebody in the house, don't you?"

"I agree that it certainly sounded like it. But I'm not used to these country noises. I suppose it could have been some sort of steady noise on the roof or close by that we haven't identified. The doors don't give the impression of having been tampered with."

"I was just afraid you were going to say something like that," said Nelson in disgust. "And if I keep talking, you'll say that maybe Condor was barking at some sort of wild animal. You never want to be sure of anything. Well, I'm telling you one thing. I'm *sure* somebody was in the house."

With that, Nelson climbed into bed and turned over noisily.

CHAPTER 11

WHAT THEY FOUND AT THE CISTERN

THE BOYS WERE UP EARLY in the morning, but when they tried to wash they found the faucets dry.

"What goes here?" Nelson demanded. "Did the well run dry? There was water enough last night."

"I guess we must have used it all—or someone did. I expect it's not a water shortage but because the power's off. They probably have an electric pump which fills a tank up on the roof."

"Maybe so," Nelson agreed, "but I don't think we could have used all that water. Well, what do we do about catching Marty? Is it about time to milk the cows?"

"I suppose so. Let's see how we'd better go about it. Can you get into the barn from the other side?"

"Sure, through those big doors where the haying wagons come in. I don't think they're locked."

The barn had been constructed against a hill, so that the big wagons or tractors could drive directly into the "upstairs," while the stables were down below.

"Then suppose you do that," Ted suggested. "Sneak around so that he won't see you coming. Meanwhile I'll busy myself out in the farmyard, as though I didn't have a thought in the world about going out to the barn. In fact, I'll see if I can't scare up some water. I'll give you about fifteen minutes, then I'll go over to the barn and into the stables. You'll be guarding the stairs inside, and we should have Marty cornered between us."

Nelson agreed to the plan, and set off, taking a long, circuitous route out of sight of anyone watching inside the barn. Consulting his watch, Ted set about his duties. As he had expected, the well was housed within a little shed in order to protect the electric pump. However, it could also be operated by hand, and he proceeded to pump a pailful of water and carry it back to the house. Condor had stayed with him for a while, but soon had pranced off. The disturbance during the night no longer troubled him.

Ted waited in the kitchen until the fifteen minutes were up, then went outside and strode toward the barn, marching directly into the stables. All their precautions had been unnecessary, for he found Nelson already down in the stable talking to Marty who was busy at the milking. Marty looked up cordially as Ted came in.

"Hi, there, Ted," he called. "Come out to help with the milking?" His clothing was wrinkled and wisps of hay clung to him, but he seemed in good spirits.

"You seem to be doing all right without me," Ted replied cheerfully, for the milk was flowing steadily into the pail.

"I was just asking him," Nelson broke in, "why he didn't come into the house last night."

"Oh, I was comfortable enough in the barn," Marty returned. "I thought I'd better stick out here till I saw whether you fellows were coming back or not. But I was planning on coming in to breakfast. There was no use trying to hide any longer, after you two bloodhounds got on my trail."

Ted's eyes narrowed. "Then you didn't come into the house last night and go upstairs—for something?"

"Of course not. Why should I?"

"But didn't you hear the dog barking?"

"Oh, yes, I heard that and I got up to look out. He must have spotted a weasel or something. He always acts that way when he sees any small animal. The people who gave him to my aunt and uncle said he used to be a hunting dog, and I suppose he never forgot it."

"Someone came into the house last night," asserted Nelson. "I heard him come up the stairs, and then go back down again."

"Did you hear it, too, Ted?"

"Not the first part. But then Nelson woke me up, and I did hear something that sounded as if a person were going down the steps. I'm not sure about it, though. It sounded to me a little too faint and far away to be someone in the house. And we didn't hear the door click as he went out, though we were both listening closely."

"But I'm sure it was somebody in the house," said Nelson positively.

It was Marty's turn to look concerned. "Well, I don't know. I have a key and my aunt must have given you her key, but as far as I know those are the only keys. Ordinarily she bolts the doors inside as well, but of course I didn't bolt them when I went outside yesterday. I locked up after myself, since I might be anywhere about the farm, and then you came and I never did get back into the house."

"But this is an old house," Nelson argued. "I don't think those locks would prove much of a problem, if someone really wanted to break in."

"Well, I'll look the house over after breakfast, and see if I can tell whether anything is missing. I may not be able to tell for sure, though. We'll have to wait till my aunt gets home for that. Did she say when she'd be getting here?"

Ted relayed his aunt's message to him, and he seemed satisfied. He had finished with the second cow, and moved on to the last one. Ted thought it was about time to get some answers to the questions they had come so far to ask.

"Why were you hiding on us yesterday, Marty? Did you think we were after you, or something?"

Marty laughed. "Oh, no, nothing like that. But I figured you were going to ask me some questions and I didn't know how to answer you. So the easiest thing was to stay out of sight and hope you'd go away."

"But you've thought of some good answers by now?"

"No, not very good ones, I'm afraid, but I guess I'm stuck with them. You'll just have to try me and see. Just what is it you wanted to ask me?"

But Ted was a little cautious. "Exactly what did you expect me to ask you?"

"Oh, something like who was it I called on the telephone Saturday night, when I pretended to be calling for the weather report. You're pretty sharp, Ted, and I thought that while I'd put it over on you for the moment, you'd probably have some second thoughts about it. I admit, though, that I didn't expect you to drive way down here to ask me. How'd you ever find this place, anyway? I don't believe I ever told you. It wasn't any secret but I just didn't think it would matter, so I didn't tell you."

"Ted's pretty sharp," Nelson interposed. "You just admitted it yourself."

"Well, I'll say it again," said Marty with another laugh. "Finding the right farm in a wide area when you don't even know the name of the party you're looking for isn't exactly child's play."

"But you haven't told me whom you called on the phone," Ted observed.

Marty was immediately serious. "No, Ted, I haven't, and I'm afraid I'm not going to. As a matter of fact, other than satisfying your curiosity, I really don't believe it is any concern of yours. Suppose you answer a question for me. Why *did* you go to all this trouble to find me?"

"Oh, we've got more questions than that one to ask you," Nelson put in. "Go to it, Ted."

Ted began very slowly, "Marty, you met me at the office on Saturday afternoon. I presume you came into Forestdale by bus. Is that correct?"

"Of course, Ted. How else would I have come? What difference does it make anyway?"

"Then you walked over to the newspaper office, where you met me. Is that also correct?"

"Perfectly correct, Ted. What about it?"

"What if I told you," said Ted deliberately, "that there are certain people who claim that you didn't walk—that you actually got a ride over to the office?"

"I'd say they were lying, of course. But suppose someone had given me a lift, why would that be a federal case?"

"It might be a federal case, after all," said Nelson warningly, but Ted made a motion to him to be quiet.

"Then you're sure that you walked all the way?"

"Of course I'm sure, Ted. Do you want me to take an oath on it? I would if I had to." He thought Ted was joking, but saw by the boys' faces that it was no joke. "You mean that maybe I *will* have to take an oath on it?"

"It just might come to that," Ted admitted. "All right, we'll say that you walked over to the office. You were carrying your suitcase?"

"Of course. It couldn't walk by itself."

"Then did anything happen along the way?"

"Nothing that I can recall."

"What about that accident where the dog was almost hit?"

"Oh—oh, yes, I remember that now. But he wasn't hit, so what difference does it make?"

"What were you doing when the accident happened?"

"Look, Ted, I couldn't have hit the dog with a car while I was walking. Oh, all right, I'll try to tell you. Let's see, a fellow in a blue Pontiac drew up to the curb and called to me. He asked me for some directions, and I stood there for a few minutes talking to him. Then there was the sound of this truck stopping suddenly—and believe me that was loud. For a moment I thought it was going to hit the Pontiac, but it didn't. So we both looked up to see what was happening. Then I exchanged a few more words with this fellow and walked on. That's all."

"What about your suitcase?" Nelson demanded. "The witnesses say they saw you taking your suitcase out of the car."

"That's silly. I remember now, he threw open his door and I stuck my head inside to talk with him, resting my suitcase partly on the floor of the car. That certainly isn't the same thing as taking my suitcase out of the car."

"Are you sure he couldn't have switched suitcases on you?"

"Switched suitcases? What for? And how could he have done it? He would have had to have another suitcase available exactly like mine, and anyway I would have discovered the difference when I opened my suitcase later. Besides, I doubt if I even took my hand off the handle of my suitcase, although it's possible that I did in the excitement of that near crash. Now would you mind telling me why you're so interested in that car?"

He stared at the others challengingly, but there was no immediate response. Presently the bewilderment left his face and was replaced with an expression of awe.

"Oh-oh. Wait a minute. The wheels are starting to churn inside. You think that man in the Pontiac was Grover Hale, don't you?"

"Well—was he?" Ted wanted to know.

"I don't know—I didn't think so before. I remember that while I sat in Nelson's car that night listening to the police broadcast, the thought flashed through my mind that it may have been Hale. But I immediately dismissed it. There was nothing at all furtive about the man I talked to. He was very pleasant and easy going. If the police were after him, would he stop to talk so casually with a stranger?"

"What did he talk to you about?"

"I remember first he asked me where Callinger Road was, and I told him I didn't know—I was a stranger there myself. Then we got to talking about its being a nice little town, and stuff like that, I don't remember it all, but I'm sure nothing at all important was said. Then there was the accident, and later I went on my way."

"And you don't know where he went?"

"Callinger Road, I suppose, wherever that is."

"It's the road between Forestdale and North Ridge. Most people don't call it by its name any more, because it has a route number. And it's about ten miles long. You don't know whom he wanted to see on Callinger Road, do you?"

"No, and I'm not even sure that he wanted to see anybody. He may simply have wanted to know where the road was that would take him to North Ridge. Anyway, he didn't tell me anything more about his business, and I didn't ask."

They stood in a silent group for a minute. Marty looked uncomfortable, as though his friends were accusing him. He had finished with the milking, and he led the way out of the barn, carrying the pails of milk with him. He took it inside a milk shed, from which he soon emerged.

"Look, fellows, would it help any if I pledged my most solemn word of honor that I didn't have anything to do with that fellow in the Pontiac, other than the little conversation I told you about?"

"What about the fellow you called on the telephone that night?" asked Ted. "You went out to meet him later, didn't you?"

"Yes, I did. But I pledge to you that what I did that night had nothing at all to do with that bank case." He thought about it for a brief time. "No, wait a minute. I'll have to withdraw that pledge. What I want to say is that *as far as I know* there is no connection between the man I met that night and Grover Hale. If there was anything between them, it would be an extraordinary coincidence, and it had nothing at all to do with me."

"I understood you to say once that you didn't know anyone in Forestdale except Nelson and me."

"That's right, Ted. I did say it. But I'll have to stand by the statement I just made, and stop right there. It isn't that I think it's none of your business—it's that I don't think it's any of my business, either. It concerns another person, and unless I had that person's permission, I wouldn't feel free to talk about it."

They were forced to leave the matter at that. Marty was a mild-mannered person, but he could be pushed only so far. Once he had taken a position which he felt was right and fair, he could not be budged.

"Well, what do we do now?" asked Nelson, trying to relieve the tension between them and Marty.

"I think the first thing is to get that generator working," Marty decided. "I won't have any trouble there. Then we can cook some breakfast. There isn't much you can do without electricity—and water."

"What happened to the water?" Ted inquired. "There seemed to be plenty last night, and we didn't use much."

"I drew it off this morning when I watered the stock. There's a tank up on the roof that is filled every day, or twice a day as needed. As soon as I get the generator humming, I'll fill it up again."

"How can you tell when it's full?" asked Ted, peering upward at the house.

"We've got the latest electronic gadgets. Can you tell where the tank is? It's right up there. And you see that very small pipe extending outward? That's the overflow pipe. You watch while the pump's working, and as soon as you see water starting to come out there you turn off the pump. Isn't science wonderful?"

"Isn't that the pump over there, on the other side of the house?" asked Nelson, somewhat puzzled.

"Oh, no, that's a cistern. Rain water collects in there. It's open, and shallower than the well. You can't be sure the water isn't contaminated, though of course it's suitable for watering the garden. Come on, I'll show you."

He led the way past the house and a short distance beyond, then stopped suddenly in his tracks. He pointed silently at the ground. There was a trail of a man's footprints, leading away from the cistern.

CHAPTER 12

THE MAN WHO GOT WET

MARTY AND NELSON pushed forward, but Ted called a warning to them.

"Wait! Don't mess up those prints. We may need them."

Approaching more carefully, the three of them stood quite close to the prints, and leaned over to examine them. But there was nothing about the prints to identify them, nor was there any explanation of why they were there. There was a stone slab around the cistern. Beyond that the ground had been turned to mud by the night's rain, and while crossing this the man had made half a dozen prints. Then he had reached the gravel path where the footprints no longer could be seen.

"Why footprints going *away* from the cistern?" asked Nelson in perplexity. "What about the footprints going *to* the cistern? He didn't drop out of a helicopter, did he?"

"It's as if he came up out of the ground and walked away," said Marty, just as puzzled as Nelson.

"I think I know what may have happened," said Ted slowly. "He didn't fly to the cistern, or anything like that. He walked there. But he must have walked there before the rain, and if he did make any footprints in the dust, they were washed out later. But by the time he left, he had to walk through the mud. The rain must have been over by then, or close to it. Otherwise it would have washed out these prints, too."

"You're only answering one mystery by making another," Nelson returned. "Why would somebody stand out here during that rainstorm? What did he want with this old cistern, anyway?"

"I don't know," said Ted thoughtfully. "I can see why somebody might get rid of something by tossing it down an old cistern. But that would only take a few seconds. There wouldn't be any reason to stand out here during the whole storm. I'm afraid I slept too soundly to hear it rain. Did you fellows hear it?"

"I did," said Nelson promptly. "Remember I told you I thought I heard footsteps, like somebody climbing the stairs? Well, to tell you the truth, I really only half heard it—*that* time. I was just about half-awake, and then it started to rain and I dozed off again. Afterward another noise woke me, and then we *both* heard those footsteps, very distinctly, going down the steps."

"I heard the rain, too," Marty agreed. "It was one of those very short but heavy downpours. It sounded like a cloudburst, coming down on the roof of that old barn. But it ended very soon, and only a little while after that Condor began to bark."

Nelson looked at Marty with some skepticism. "Look here, Marty, I don't want to accuse anybody of anything, but—are you sure these aren't *your* footprints?"

"Of course not," said Marty indignantly. "As far as I know, I've never walked in my sleep, and I certainly would know it if I got soaking wet. For that matter, how do I know they're not *your* footprints? Oh, look, I don't mean that, really, but just for the sake of everybody's peace of mind, let's *all* make our footprints in the mud."

This seemed fair enough, and each of the boys made a careful footprint alongside those of the mysterious intruder. Ted's and Nelson's were immediately ruled out, and they had brought no spare shoes along. Marty's were a little closer, but still they were slightly longer and narrower than the prints of the prowler. While he might have had a spare pair of shoes, it was unlikely he would have had them out in the barn with him. Furthermore his clothes, though they looked as if he had slept in the hay, did not indicate he had been out in a downpour during the night. Ted and Nelson claimed they were fully satisfied.

"Now breakfast!" Marty cried. "I'll go after that generator, and you see what you can scare up to put on the stove when the current comes on. I'm starved!"

He hurried off, while Ted and Nelson walked more slowly toward the kitchen.

"How about that, Ted?" asked Nelson in a low voice. "Are you satisfied that Marty is telling the truth?"

"I want to believe him," Ted responded slowly. "He pledged his word of honor on part of his story, and I'm surely going to believe him on that, until I have good reason not to."

"I know, I'd like to believe it, too, Ted. But remember that you've got a handful of witnesses who will claim they saw him getting out of that car. And he hasn't told you the name of the man he met during that night. A few other things don't quite add up, either. But suppose he is telling the truth, what are we going to do about those witnesses? If it ever comes to court, that's going to be pretty strong evidence against him. We've got to find some way to protect him, if we can."

"Well, I suppose the story of the witnesses is reasonable enough. They saw Marty with his head inside the open door of the car resting his suitcase just as he said. When he straightened up with the suitcase in his hand, it could look as if he were getting out of the car. The trouble is that no one noticed him beforehand. They only spotted him because of the incident with the dog. I suppose a good defense attorney might be able to discredit the story of the witnesses."

"Not very easily, when it's nine against one. I'm assuming that those two witnesses you didn't interview will tell the same stories, and of course we're all discounting that one woman. She couldn't be right." Nelson hesitated a moment before going on. "But I've got to say that as much as I like Marty, and as much as I would be willing to rely on his word, I think there's one thing he's not telling us. I think he's got a pretty good idea who the man is that made these tracks!"

Ted looked at him narrowly. "That's crazy, Nel. No matter what he's up to, he isn't going to give some man permission to ransack his aunt's house."

"Then what's your idea about those footprints?"

"I don't have a very good idea. I've got a hazy notion that the man may have been trying to fish something *out* of that cistern. That would take a good deal longer than simply dropping something in."

"But during a rainstorm? That would be a heck of a time to do it."

"Maybe it was the best possible time. I think the rain drove Condor back into his doghouse, so that for a little while, at least, he didn't have to worry about that. Say what you want to, this Condor makes a better pet than he does a watchdog, and even a dog is going to look out for his own comfort."

"You think he found what he was after?"

"Who knows? I don't suppose dredging up something like that would be easy. Then when the dog spotted him, he had to beat it."

"What about those footsteps we heard inside the house?"

"Well, that's something I can't explain, unless there were two of them."

"Are you going to tell Marty what you think about this?"

Ted hesitated. "No, not right away, anyhow. He's full of some problem of his own that he isn't telling us about. Until we're sure he's being open with us, I don't see any reason why we should open up to him."

They had reached the kitchen by this time. Ted scouted around until he found some bacon to fry and some pancake batter to mix up. The electricity came on, water was available at the faucet, and Ted put Nelson to work cooking the pancakes.

"How do you stand with the newspaper?" asked Nelson, bending over his task with critical concentration for a stove of this type was new to him, and he was only a novice cook, anyway.

"I'm going to call Mr. Dobson, right after breakfast."

"Why don't you call him now?"

"I don't care much for this rural telephone service. You never know who may be listening in. I'll go somewhere where there's dial service. There's no use getting this Grover Hale business all over the neighborhood."

"You think Mr. Dobson will let you stay on the story? After all, these footprints and the rest of it don't seem to have anything to do with Hale and the bank, and that's the story you're supposed to be working on."

"I think I can talk him into letting me stay on, at least for another day. After all, Marty is the missing witness in the Grover Hale case, and so there is a link."

"But just what is Marty a witness to? It seems to me the only way he could be a witness is if he and Hale were in the business together. Marty could only be a witness against himself. Of course if he were just an innocent bystander, he might still know something that would help us find Hale, but that chance seems to have gone glimmering."

"He can testify that Hale didn't act like a fugitive. I know that's a rather feeble kind of testimony, but it might turn out to be important."

Marty came in a few minutes later, and the boys sat down to a hearty breakfast. That is, Ted and Marty did, but Nelson was kept busy making more pancakes until there were plenty for all. Then Ted said he had an errand to do.

"Take my car," Nelson offered. "I trust your driving."

"All right, if you're sure you don't want to come along."

"No, thanks. I imagine there are plenty of things around here that I can help Marty with."

"You sure can," Marty admitted. "I'd like to get everything in tiptop shape before my aunt gets back, if I can. It'll give her fewer things to fuss about."

Ted drove off, and put through his call. He gave Mr. Dobson a careful summary of everything that had happened since he had left Forestdale the previous day.

"Then you don't really think Martin Blaine has anything to do with Grover Hale?"

"I don't think so, Mr. Dobson. It was just a harmless sidewalk conversation that everybody misinterpreted. But I wish I could stay on here a little longer. I think Marty is protecting someone, and the only person I can think of would be his aunt. We're expecting her home from the hospital today, and then we may learn a little bit more about this. She's rather poor, but her husband was a minister and quite prominent in the neighborhood—and this is in our circulation area, so maybe there will be a story down here of a different kind."

"All right, Ted, stick with it. I'll expect that you'll either be back here, or call in, before our Thursday noon deadline."

"Thank you, Mr. Dobson."

"Oh, one more thing, Ted. Ken Kutler called this morning. He reached your mother last night, but she didn't give him much satisfaction, so he called the office today. When he didn't find you here either, I'm sure he put two and two together and figures you're out of town on this Grover Hale yarn."

"Did he leave a message for me?"

"Yes, he said he had called those other two witnesses, and they had virtually corroborated the stories of the previous witnesses. They, too, claim that they saw a young man with a suitcase getting out of Grover Hale's car."

"Which never happened," said Ted.

"Maybe not. People often see what they expect to see. Kutler said he'd give you a complete rundown on them *when you have time*. He accented those last words. He's pretty sharp competition, Ted. I've got more than half a notion that he's following some lead of his own on the same case."

"Well, I'm glad he called, though I knew he would. He always keeps a promise like that. Is that all, Mr. Dobson?"

"That's all, Ted. Good luck."

When Ted returned to Meadows, he found Marty and Nelson busy with farm chores. But Nelson gave him a slight wink behind Marty's back, and Ted knew that something had happened while he was gone. He got Nelson alone as soon as he could.

"That Marty," said Nelson, shaking his head. "As soon as you were gone, he did his best to get me out of here. He got up a list of supplies and hinted pretty strongly that he'd like me to go after them in Mrs. Martin's car. He didn't want to go himself, he said, because he was waiting for a call from the hospital. Oh, he made it sound very plausible, but somehow I couldn't avoid feeling that the whole thing was just a stunt for getting me away from the farm."

"What did you do?"

"Of course I said I'd go. I took the car, and drove off down the road a little way. Then I sneaked back by foot, just to see what he was up to while I was gone. I found out, all right. Don't point it out, but you see that big shed across the field?"

"Yes. What is it?"

"I think it's called the sugar house. It's where they boil the maple sap into sugar in the spring. I don't think it's used very much the rest of the year. Well, as soon as he thought I was gone, he headed straight over there."

"What do you think?"

"What can I think? I'm pretty sure he's meeting somebody there."

"The man who made the footprints at the cistern?"

"Who else?"

Ted thought it over carefully. "Well, what do you think we'd better do about it?"

"You'd better decide. You're the captain of this crew. You're the one with a job to lose."

"Well, I don't exactly like to plunge into anything I don't understand, but I would like a chance to look around there. Maybe after . . ."

The telephone rang, and Marty, who was closer to the house than they were, ran for the building. The phone rang nine or ten times before he got to it, but people in the country expect this sort of thing, and are in no hurry to hang up. A minute or two later Marty came out of the house.

"That was the hospital," he called. "They're discharging my aunt. They want me to come and pick her up right now."

He washed and changed and was ready to leave fifteen minutes later.

"We'll be back for dinner, so don't bother fixing anything first," he advised them. "My aunt will want to fix us something decent, as she calls it. She doesn't think much of college-boy menus."

They waved as he drove off. Nelson was anxious to get down to the sugar house, but took the precaution of hurrying down to the road first to make sure that Marty really had taken off. He had no intention of falling victim to the same sort of maneuver that he had tried successfully on Marty. Then he and Ted started across the field, Condor bounding along not far from their side.

"Let's try to make this sort of casual," was Ted's idea. "We'll just wander past, and if Condor sniffs anything, I'm sure he'll let us know. If he doesn't we can go right into the sugar house, and see if we can discover anything."

"Huh, Condor's probably made friends with this man by now. He was with Marty this morning. Suppose the man's still there? Do we want to get involved openly?"

"I'd rather not—not until we've had a chance to talk with Mrs. Martin. Maybe she and Marty will tell us everything this afternoon. But if there is a man there, he'll probably spot us and we may not have any choice. Want to back out?"

"No, thanks. I'm with you."

They walked past the sugar house, and Condor showed no unusual alarm or even very much interest in it. They walked on a short way, then returned. Resolutely, Ted pushed open the door, but there was no one inside. In looking the place over, however, they spotted some cigar butts on the floor.

"Recent, too," was Nelson's opinion.

There was no doubt that a man had been there, and Marty had kept an appointment with him. They looked around carefully for footprints, hoping they might find something to match up with the footprints by the cistern, but found nothing distinctive enough to do them any good. Somewhat dissatisfied, they left the shack and headed back toward the farmhouse to wait for Marty and Mrs. Martin.

CHAPTER 13

A REUNION

MARTY made good time, and returned with his aunt before noon. She greeted Ted and Nelson cordially, and then said she wanted to put her things away and begin preparation of their meal.

"Did Marty tell you that someone entered the house last night?" asked Nelson, wondering if Marty had indeed mentioned it. He might not have wanted to worry his aunt, or he might know more about the man at the cistern than he cared to say, but Nelson was bluntly determined upon a showdown.

"Yes, he did. I certainly can't imagine what he was after. I wouldn't keep valuables about the house—even if I had anything I could consider a valuable." She laughed. "But I'll look around and see if anything is missing."

"He might have been in the house as long as half an hour," Nelson pointed out. "I thought I heard him, then it rained and I fell asleep, then I woke up again."

"Well, half an hour ought to give him time to do some pretty thorough searching. I'll see if anything looks disturbed. I'm a pretty careful housekeeper in my way, and I think I'd know it if any clumsy man went through my possessions."

She looked around the ground floor, then went upstairs. When she came down again, she assured them that she could find no indication that any strange person had been in the house.

"I've looked in all my closets and drawers and on the shelves, and I'm quite certain no one has disturbed anything. And those are the places where something would be hidden—if I had anything to hide."

She appeared to be placing no faith at all in Nelson's story of the intruder. But was she telling the truth? Even Ted wondered. He wanted to believe her, but he had noticed a certain rather odd restraint between her and Marty. Possibly she was covering up for him. At least Ted was certain they had had a long talk on the way back from the hospital, and had reached certain decisions which would not be revealed till later.

When they had finished dinner Mrs. Martin said:

"I've some clearing up in the kitchen to do, and Marty has some chores. But will you all be in the living room at two o'clock? There are some things that Marty and I want to tell you."

At two o'clock they sat down to their little conference.

"Marty and I talked it over," she announced, "and we decided that there wasn't any further use in hiding anything from you. Marty has been trying to spare my feelings, and in so doing he has only got himself in deeper. I'm sure you must suspect him of all sorts of things which aren't true.

"My husband, who, as you know, was a minister and a fine, respected man, died about a year ago. Among his papers I found this item."

She held out a canceled check for them to examine. Dated about two years ago, it was made out in the amount of fifty dollars, payable to Ernest Crowell, and was signed by Mr. Martin. After they had all examined it, it was returned to her.

"I never looked at my husband's papers while he was living. Even if I had, I wouldn't have known what this check was for. My husband, of course, was a recipient of many confidences from the people who trusted him, and in return he gave them the best advice he could. He rarely discussed any of these confidences with me, and I didn't want to know them unless there was some way I could help. I know that people would sometimes give him money with instructions to relay it to someone else, and he always did so. I might have thought this check was for something of that nature, except for two other things.

"My husband had been on a short trip near Stanton about the time this check was drawn. When he returned from this trip, his car was damaged, but the damages had been repaired. He never mentioned the matter to me, doubtless because he did not want to worry me. I was somewhat concerned about his driving in his last years.

"The second incident occurred just before he died. He had been in a coma for several days, but near the end he rallied a little and recovered his senses. One of the things he said to me was, 'Karen, I didn't tell you about it before, but be sure to pay off that Ernest Crowell note.' I promised.

"Naturally, at the first opportunity I went through all his papers, resolved to keep my last promise to him. I did not find a copy of the note—the original would, of course, be in the hands of the payee—and the only reference to Ernest Crowell I could find was in the check which you have seen. I made inquiries among my husband's friends, and at the bank where this check was cashed, but I was unable to find out where Mr. Crowell lived. Putting two and two together, I decided that this note had something to do with the accident my husband had had about that time. But I did not know how much money was due Mr. Crowell, or how I could reach him. The only thing I could do, it seemed, was to wait for Mr. Crowell to get in touch with me. Meanwhile, I saved up all the money I could to meet the note. As you may have noticed, the farm has been getting run down. There are many things that should be done around here, but I have been afraid to do them because I might need the money for the note.

"About six months ago, Mr. Crowell came out to the farm. I must tell you that I felt very sorry for him. He has a very bad limp, a hip injury, which he said was the result of the accident. Just in case you think he may have been faking his injury, I can assure you he wasn't. I had some nurse's training before my marriage, and I can tell when people are in pain but are trying to hide it. That was what Mr. Crowell was doing.

"He was very nice about the whole thing. He said that Mr. Martin had missed a payment on his note, and he had come out here to see what had happened. He knew that my husband was a minister, and that money was always a problem with him, and while he didn't want to put any pressure on him he could use the money. He was greatly disturbed when I told him of my husband's death, and said just to forget the whole thing. But I told him about my promise to my husband, and my determination to pay the note. Finally he brought out the note and showed it to me. It was for fifteen thousand dollars! Well, you can imagine how shocked I was by this. There was of course no way I could raise such a sum except by selling the farm, and I decided this was what I would have to do."

"Oh, no, Aunt Karen," Marty objected. "You mustn't ever sell this farm. That isn't what Uncle Mike wanted for you."

"He wanted me to pay that note," his aunt reminded him.

"Are you sure the note was genuine?" asked Ted suspiciously.

"Oh, yes, there was no doubt at all that it was my husband's signature. I asked him how much my husband had paid on the note, and he said just the fifty dollars, which was all he had had available at the time of the accident. This, of course, was proved by the canceled check. He said that my husband had promised to pay him five hundred dollars every six months, although this was only an oral promise. Since the note was written, I suppose legally he could have demanded payment for the whole amount whenever he wished. Oh, I don't consider the amount my husband had agreed to pay him as exorbitant considering the terrible injury he had received, and I know that this must have been a matter that was weighing heavily on my husband's mind during his long illness. I talked with Mr. Crowell about the accident and he told me when it had happened—it corresponded with the time of my husband's trip—and he even told me the name of the garage where his car had been repaired. Just to be on the safe side, I inquired of the garage, and it proved to be so."

"Did you pay Mr. Crowell any money?" asked Ted.

"I gave him two hundred dollars. It was all I could spare at the time. I told him I would try to pay him the rest as soon as I could, but I didn't see how I could do it until I had sold the farm. Then I would work out a final settlement with him."

"Didn't you think of consulting a lawyer?" Nelson inquired.

She turned to him. "No, Nelson, I thought it better not to. For one thing, people of our persuasion do not believe in taking legal measures against members of our own flock, and he said he was of our persuasion. Then there was the undoubted fact that my husband felt this obligation, and that I had given him my irrevocable promise to meet it. And Mr. Crowell was being very nice about it. I practically had to force him to take the two hundred dollars, and he said he hoped I wouldn't sell the farm. Perhaps something else could be worked out. He said he would never have come out here at all, if he had known of my husband's death."

"Do you know Mr. Crowell's address now?" Ted took up the questioning.

"Yes, he lives in Stanton. As a matter of fact I had to mail the two hundred dollars to him, since I had to get a check from the bank. I no longer have an active checking account."

"Then that was the last time you saw Mr. Crowell?"

"Yes, that was the last *I* saw of him, but now it's time for Marty to take up the story." She leaned back in her chair.

"I got a letter from Mr. Crowell a few weeks before the college term ended," Marty proceeded. "He didn't tell me exactly what the trouble was, but he let me know that my late uncle had owed him a substantial sum of money. He wondered if he could talk to me sometime about it privately. I told him that I would be stopping off in Forestdale on my way out to the farm, and he said that would be an excellent place to meet me. He gave me a number to call, and as you know I called it late last Saturday night—he had told me that he would be late getting in. As it turned out, the number was that of the hotel. I would have met him there, but he said it would be simpler for him to drive over. He drew up a few doors from the house, and as soon as I thought Ted and his mother were asleep, I got up and went down to meet him. I didn't want to make a big mystery out of this, Ted, but at that time I thought there might be something which would hurt my uncle's reputation, so of course I wanted to keep as quiet as I could about it, until I knew the story.

"We sat in Mr. Crowell's car—and first let me say I agree entirely with my aunt. Mr. Crowell was not faking his injuries. He told me then about the accident, and how my aunt wanted to sell her farm, but he was anxious to avoid hurting her. He asked me if I thought I could work out a settlement with him, and then we could go to my aunt and tell her everything was settled and she wouldn't have to sell. We wouldn't even have to tell her the amount of the settlement, which would be less than the full amount due, so that she would feel she had carried out her promise to her husband. You probably know that I would do anything in the world for my aunt and uncle. They were the closest things to parents that I can ever remember. I have very little money, but I'll come into some property from my parents in a few months. It's not a great deal, but it would have seen me through college and started on a career. I would be glad to use it for my aunt and for the memory of my uncle if necessary."

"Oh, Marty!" Mrs. Martin interjected, "I could never let you do anything like that for me."

"Why not? It's nothing more than you would do for me. However," he continued, "I wasn't going to hand over my inheritance to the first man who came along and said, 'Your uncle owed me some money—gimme.' I told him that when I came into my property I'd have to consult with an attorney and make sure the proper papers were signed. I didn't want to make a settlement with him on the basis of part of the amount, and then have him go back to my aunt for the rest of it. He said he didn't like the idea of lawyers, but he'd think it over. We made an appointment to meet in the sugar house this morning. When I saw those footprints by the cistern this morning, I had a pretty good notion it was Mr. Crowell who made them. But I had no idea what he could have been doing around the cistern—then. I've got a better one now.

"I met Mr. Crowell in the sugar house this morning. He sort of hemmed and hawed around, and said he'd been examining his conscience, and felt that the idea of lawyers would be a violation of his religious scruples. But he said that there was one thing I could do for him. It seems relations between my uncle and himself had developed closely, and various confidences had been exchanged. There were certain things about himself that he didn't care to reveal, and he had made certain arrangements with my uncle. He couldn't give me the details, but the gist of it was that my uncle had a certain key of his. After Mr. Crowell had made amends, this key was to be returned to him. He wanted me to give him that key now.

"Naturally I asked him what the key was for, and he said he couldn't tell me that, but I suppose it is the key to a safe deposit box, or something of that sort which contains money or stocks and bonds. I asked him how I could be sure the key was really his, and he said that he had told me about it, hadn't he, and no one else had claimed it. I then asked him how I could be sure he had done what my uncle thought he should, and he said he guessed I'd just have to take his word for that. I told him that I didn't know anything about such a key, but that if it was his, he could be sure it would be returned to him. But the first thing to do was to find the key, after which we could talk about it again."

"And I suppose you don't know anything about such a key?" Ted inquired, turning to Mrs. Martin.

She shook her head. "No, I never heard of it, until Marty mentioned it on the way home from the hospital. Of course I have my husband's key ring, but I know all those keys. Now I've no doubt that there are other keys lying around loose in the house, keys that don't belong to anything any more. But I'm sure that if this was a valuable key as Mr. Crowell suggested, my husband would never have been so careless with it. He would have put it away securely where he could find it again, some place where it wouldn't get accidentally thrown out."

"What about the person who came into the house last night?" asked Nelson suddenly. "Don't you think he may have been searching for a key?"

"I might think so, Nelson," said Mrs. Martin slowly, "except that I can't see any evidence that a very careful search was made."

"Also at the very time Nelson claims he was hearing footsteps in the house," Marty asserted, "Mr. Crowell was probably outside fooling around with that old cistern." He turned to Ted. "What do you think about this?"

Ted got slowly to his feet. "Before I say anything else, is it all right if I make a phone call? There's only one hotel in Forestdale, and I want to see if Mr. Crowell was really registered there on Saturday."

"He must have been," Marty pointed out. "I called him there. The number is Forestdale 2222, and I asked for room 315."

"Yes, I recall the number. My point is that if Mr. Crowell was there on legitimate business, he would probably use his own name, and if his business was shady, he would probably register under an alias. Want me to try it?"

"He must have used the right name," Mrs. Martin interposed. "He said he was of our persuasion."

"Of course he'd say that," said Marty. "Let Ted call."

Ted put through the call, and after a short conversation he hung up.

"That room was registered under the name of a Mr. Grant. I can give you my opinion now. I think Mr. Crowell is one of the smoothest confidence workers we are ever likely to run up against, and that we'd better decide right now what we're going to do about him."

CHAPTER 14

THE FREEDOM RAILROAD

THE OTHERS expected Ted to continue, but instead he turned to Nelson.

"You're pretty shrewd, Nel, when it comes to smelling out skulduggery. What do you think about Mr. Crowell?"

Nelson considered carefully. "Well, his story about the accident and about Mr. Martin owing him some money might be *partly* true—he's got some proof to back it up. But I think his story about this key he's looking for smells from here to the nearest satellite. I don't know whom he thinks he's kidding about that."

Ted resumed, "I agree that there might be some truth in the accident part of it, but I don't think it's entirely true, either. The most suspicious thing is the way he shies away whenever the subject of lawyers is mentioned. Mrs. Martin thinks it's due to religious conviction, but it could also be due to the fact that he doesn't want anyone looking too closely into his affairs. I think the amount of money he claims is owing to him—fifteen thousand dollars—is interesting, too. A thousand dollars a year represents just about the very most he could expect to collect, and fifteen years is just about the longest possible period of time. Then when he came to try to collect it, he found he couldn't and Mrs. Martin would have to sell the farm. For all his reluctance to accept money from you, Mrs. Martin, I have to point out to you that he *did* take your money—all the money you were able to spare. These confidence men usually have a smooth, modest, reluctant air, but they end up by getting what they want—the successful ones do.

"Then, when he saw he couldn't get anything more out of you, he went to Marty. But he soon saw he would run into the same obstacle—lawyers. He immediately dropped his demands on Marty. I don't know exactly what lawyers could find out about him. They can't examine a man's conscience, but at the very least they might look up his church membership, and find out that he isn't a member of your faith after all. I know you want to be fair, Mrs. Martin, but I don't believe you should pay Mr. Crowell another penny, at least until we find out that he really was hurt in an accident with your husband. Then I'd get the whole thing down on paper, in some kind of legal form."

"Can't we find out about the accident?" Nelson spoke up. "According to the law in this state, all accidents are supposed to be reported."

"Yes, but I understand the law was poorly enforced up until this year, and it is even possible that Mr. Martin wasn't familiar with it. At any rate, we do know that every little fender scrape isn't reported to the police, and so it's often hard to know just where to draw the line. And even if there was a police report on it, we don't know just where the accident happened, or the exact time, so it might be difficult to look up. I'd put the burden of proof on Mr. Crowell. Make *him* show just where the accident happened, and when, and how badly he was injured."

"He does have some proof," Marty pointed out. "He's got that note signed by Uncle Mike."

"Yes, but even so I'd like to know how the amount of damages was calculated, and why no police record was made, if it wasn't."

"Aren't we forgetting," Mrs. Martin put in, "that he's not asking for any more money?"

"Yes, what about that key he wants me to get for him?" Marty questioned. "Does he really want a key? If so, what does he want it for? And if not, why did he make up a story like that?"

"And the cistern business, too," Nelson added. "Maybe he did think the key was in the cistern. I suppose he might have been trying to dredge up something from the bottom with a scoop or pail. Or maybe he had a magnet on a rope, and was hoping he could fish up the key with that."

"He probably wouldn't get it that way," Marty replied. "There must be a lot of sludge at the bottom, and if the key was there very long it would be pretty well buried in it."

"Well, maybe it wasn't the best way of getting it," Nelson answered, "but he might try that first. Has that cistern ever been cleaned out? Would it be very expensive to do?"

"No," Mrs. Martin replied, "it's never been cleaned out as long as we've lived on the farm. I suppose it could be done, if necessary, but it would probably take a while, and there'd be some expense."

"And then you might not find the key, even if it had been there," Marty went on. "I don't think a cleaning job would be that thorough. Anyway, suppose we did find the key—or at least found some key— what would we do with it? And if we didn't find it, we'd be no better off than we are now."

"And what about the footsteps I heard in the house last night?" Nelson questioned. "I don't see how Mr. Crowell could have been out fooling with the cistern and inside the house at the same time."

"That is a little difficult to figure out," Ted admitted. He turned to Mrs. Martin. "Do you know of anyone, other than Mr. Crowell, who might have had some reason for breaking into the house?"

"Well, no, not really. But I can remember one rather strange happening last year. I got a letter from a man I had never heard of. He asked me in a rather urgent way whether among my late husband's papers I had found any mention of his name. I wrote back to tell him that I hadn't. I suppose that he had confided some misdoings to my husband, and was afraid the matter might come out. I did my best to relieve his mind, and I never heard from him again."

"Do you recall his name?" asked Ted.

"No, I'm afraid not, and I purposely destroyed his letter. I prefer not to save letters which might embarrass someone in case they were found."

"How do you figure this key business out, Ted?" Nelson inquired. "Use your mathematics on it." He nodded toward Ted, while addressing himself to Marty. "He always pulls down an A in math. Let's see what those fellows can do when they're faced with a real problem."

Ted meditated. "Mr. Crowell is obviously after something. Is it a key, or is it something else? Why should he have said it was a key if it was something else? I can think of only one reason. It might be simply a cover-up, possibly to explain his snooping around here. To hide his real purpose, he dreamed up a fantastic story. On the other hand if he really did want to find a certain key, and felt that he needed

Marty's help he might have told a partial truth. But neither Marty nor Mrs. Martin know anything about any key, so I don't see how they can help him. That makes the idea of a cover-up more attractive."

"Mathematics," said Nelson, nodding his head sagely. "I don't understand it, even after he tells me the answer."

Ted laughed. "I guess it's because I really don't know the answer. I can't tell whether there is a key or not, and if there is, what it's for."

"Nobody else seems to have any better ideas about it, either," Nelson continued. "So what comes next on the program, Ted? A while ago I got the impression that maybe you intended to look up Mr. Crowell and confront him with things."

"Yes, I have been considering it. We could still drive into Stanton today, and be back here before dark. That might be the first step in trying to clear this thing up."

"Am I invited?" Martin inquired.

"It really might be better if you didn't come with us. You've had dealings with Mr. Crowell already. But he doesn't know anything about Nelson and me being down here, does he?"

"I don't think so. He may have seen someone around, but he wouldn't know you from Harvey Pierson, who's often working around here."

"Then why not let me approach him? I'll let him know I'm a reporter from the *Town Crier*, and make him think I'm following up an independent lead on the story. This way, he might at least offer me a different story from the one he gave you. It'll give us something to compare."

This plan was agreed to By everyone, and Ted and Nelson were soon out on the road, headed toward Stanton.

"And we can stop by at the Stantonville State Bank," Nelson pointed out.

"What for? It's closed until the records are audited."

"Flash your press card, and get in to talk with someone."

"I would, if I had any intelligent questions to ask. I'm afraid I haven't just yet."

Nelson gave all his attention to the driving for a few minutes. Then he said, "You know something, Ted. I asked you for your opinion about that key. I notice you didn't ask me for mine."

"Well, pardon the oversight. What is it?"

"I don't think there's any key. I didn't want to say so in front of Mrs. Martin and Marty, but I think Mr. Crowell is after something else entirely."

"Like what, for instance?"

"Like the missing loot from the Stantonville Bank."

"What! You must be crazy."

"If I am, maybe that's all to the good, because then I can guess how some other crazy person's mind might work. I didn't say the money was there. I just said that Mr. Crowell might *think* it was there."

"How do you figure that?"

"Because he's one of those smooth confidence men, and confidence men thrive on tips and rumors, and watch the papers closely for any kind of leads they can get. He must have heard by now about a young man reported getting out of Grover Hale's car, and he could easily have figured out by now that that person was Marty. He might have thought Marty was in on the robbery. Or that Marty was a friend of Hale's, and that Hale thought the farm was a good place to hide the money. Will you buy that, Ted?"

"I just might. You're my authority on crazy people."

As they approached Stanton in the late afternoon, Nelson asked:

"Have you got your interview with Mr. Crowell planned yet?"

"I've been thinking about it. It's hard to know just what to say, because I'm not sure what line he's going to take. I'll sort of play it by ear."

They passed the Stantonville State Bank, and then drove on toward the suburbs. Finding Mr. Crowell's place was no problem, for it turned out to be quite a large estate. Both boys were surprised, since it wasn't the sort of residence you'd expect for a swindler.

"Unless he's swindled an awful lot of people," Nelson decided.

"And didn't get caught at it," Ted added.

They rang the bell, and were admitted by a servant. Mr. Crowell came in, an elderly man with white hair and twinkling eyes. Ted was getting surer by the minute that something was wrong, and when he noticed that Mr. Crowell walked quite straight—although Mrs. Martin and Marty had both spoken of him as being crippled—he was certain of it. Whatever plans he had made for this interview had to be tossed out the window.

He introduced himself and Nelson, then asked:

"Were you acquainted with a minister named Michael Martin?"

"Why, yes. I met him rather unexpectedly, on one occasion. Suppose we have a spot of tea, and then you can tell me why you are interested in my brief friendship with the late Reverend Mr. Martin."

When they were seated and the tea was served, Ted continued:

"Would you mind telling me under just what circumstances you knew Mr. Martin?"

"Oh, I don't mind telling you, though I had reason to hope that the matter would never come up again. Mr. Martin owed—or thought he owed me—a small amount of money. I am a retired businessman, and as you can see, money is no particular problem with me, as it was with him. For that reason I would much have preferred to forget about it, but Mr. Martin was a man of strong conscience. I'm sure even a small debt like that would worry him greatly."

"How much money did he owe you?"

"A hundred and fifty dollars, altogether. He paid me fifty dollars of it."

"A hundred and fifty dollars! Are you sure it wasn't fifteen thousand dollars?"

"Perfectly sure, unless someone moved the decimal point."

"And that's just what someone did!" exclaimed Nelson excitedly. He had intended to let Ted do all the talking, but this revelation was too much for him. However, he let Ted resume the interview.

"Why did Mr. Martin owe you this money?"

"We ran into each other—and I mean that literally. Mr. Martin was coming out of a cross street in a little village called Tangers, about twenty miles from here. I had the right of way, but I noticed at once that a stop sign which should have been in place on the cross street had either fallen over or been knocked down by vandals. I couldn't regard Mr. Martin's offense as a very serious one, since I was not at all hurt. The front end of his car ran into the side of mine, so there was very little injury to his car, although mine was rather extensively damaged.

"I brought Mr. Martin back to my home here, and we talked it over. The damage to my car would cost between three and four hundred dollars, but Mr. Martin lived in a world considerably apart from that of business and prices, and I was able to convince him that a hundred and fifty dollars would cover everything. He wrote me a note for that amount, and a day or two later sent me fifty dollars. He said he would pay the balance as soon as he could, and I knew he wouldn't forget it. When I didn't hear from him for a long time, I figured that it was a difficult matter for him to raise even that amount. Later I learned of his illness, and then of his death."

"Didn't he carry liability insurance on his car?"

"No, it had lapsed, either through oversight or because he wasn't able to meet the premium. My car was insured against casualty, of course, but I didn't put in a claim. If I had, my insurance company would have paid for my damage, and then tried to collect the sum from Mr. Martin, which I didn't want to happen."

"Was there a police report of the accident?"

"No. Tangers is unincorporated, and as you may know it's across the state line, where there's no law requiring the reporting of accidents to the state police. Actually, I never felt that Mr. Martin owed me anything at all. As far as I am concerned, the fact that the sign post was down freed him of blame. The only reason I took the money was that I thought it would make him feel better about it. If Mrs. Martin still feels she owes me a hundred dollars, I wish you could persuade her to forget it."

"I'm afraid it isn't a matter of a hundred dollars, Mr. Crowell. It's a matter of fifteen thousand. Someone presented a note to her for this amount and asked payment. This person pretended to be Ernest Crowell, though obviously it wasn't you."

"Of course it was not my doing," Mr. Crowell said indignantly. "What a rotten thing to do."

"Do you know what happened to your note?" Ted asked.

"I presume it got shoved away in a desk drawer. If it had been thrown out, it would have been no surprise to me. As I said, I had no intention of trying to collect on it. But presumably somebody did get hold of that note, raise the amount and try to collect it. What do you know about this man who called himself Ernest Crowell?"

"Neither of us actually saw him, but he was described to us as a mild-mannered person with a very painful limp."

Mr. Crowell nodded thoughtfully, though his face had darkened. "That's Mr. Hauser, my handyman around here. He injured his hip years ago, and although I didn't know him then, I've been told that it soured his .disposition as well. He arouses a person's sympathy, and so I've kept him about the place. He could have had access to my desk, may have overheard some of my conversation with Mr. Martin and I suppose he could intercept my mail once in a while, if he wanted to. But obviously now he will have to go. Do you have any proof to back up your charges?"

"Mrs. Martin paid him two hundred dollars. I suppose you could get a receipt from her bank, showing that she paid him the money under the name of Ernest Crowell."

"Yes, I believe I could. Since he endorsed the check as Ernest Crowell, and I can prove I'm Ernest Crowell, the bank would let me see it. Well, I must thank you young men for bringing the matter to my attention. Tell Mrs. Martin I'll return her two hundred dollars."

Ted shook his head. "I'm sure she wouldn't take it from you. If Mr. Hauser decided to return it, it might be different."

"It's possible I could make him decide," Mr. Crowell said grimly.

As they were leaving, Ted noticed the huge bookcases in the room, and commented on them. Mr. Crowell removed one of the volumes to show him.

"I'm a Civil War buff. That was what Mr. Martin and I were talking about until the early hours of the morning. I told him that his house had once been a station on the Underground Railroad. It was a dangerous business, since federal law allowed slavecatchers to pursue runaway slaves into free territory and reclaim them—and sometimes they weren't too particular about declaring free Negroes to be runaways. Mr. Martin hadn't known this about his own house, but was very much interested."

On the way home, Nelson said thoughtfully: "A station on the Underground Railroad—I *knew* that house was old. But I wonder where they hid the runaway slaves? Is that where all that bank money is hidden?"

CHAPTER 15

OPERATION PITCHFORK

DURING THE NIGHT there was another alarm, as Condor barked furiously. Both Ted and Nelson woke up, and looked out the window. They could see the dog standing in the moonlight—but this time he was facing the bam rather than the cistern. They knew Condor didn't pursue something which frightened him, but simply held his ground and barked. Was there really someone in the barn?

The noise had also awakened Marty, and he came to their room and joined them at the window.

"Think there's someone out there?" Ted asked.

"Could be. There wouldn't be much trouble getting into the barn. I've locked the stable doors below, so it would be difficult to steal a cow. But the big doors upstairs can be opened. There isn't much anyone could walk away with up there."

"Why don't we go out and catch that phony Mr. Crowell red-handed?" Nelson demanded. "We'd be three against one."

"He'd probably slip by us in the dark. Anyway, I'm pretty sure it isn't Mr. Hauser. He wouldn't have any reason to come back yet. I was supposed to meet him at the sugar house Saturday morning, and I think he'd wait till he found out if I would help him."

"Unless he decided to look for that key himself," Nelson suggested. "How about that, Ted? Are we going to wait for Mr. Hauser to find the key, or are we going to hunt for it ourselves?"

"I've got no objection to doing whatever we can tomorrow—I mean today—for this may be my last day here. But how do you go about hunting for a key on a big farm? That seems worse than hunting for a needle in a haystack."

"Of course we're not sure it's a key," Marty cautioned them, "but suppose it is something small and valuable. Where could it be? It could be buried somewhere, but somehow I don't think so. My uncle might have had trouble finding it again himself, and anyway, it doesn't sound like him. It's more likely to be in one of the buildings. I think the barn is the best bet. If it was somewhere in the house, Aunt Karen would almost certainly have come across it by now."

"I still can't figure this thing out," Ted mused. "Suppose there was a valuable key, how well would your uncle hide it? Would he hide it some place where only he would be likely to find it? Or would he hide it where someone else would find it, your aunt, for instance, so she could handle it if something happened to him? But if your aunt did find it, how would she know what to do with it?"

"He might have left some directions with the key. Still, the fact is that Aunt Karen *didn't* come across that key. If it isn't in the barn, I wouldn't have any idea where to look."

"In the cistern," said Nelson promptly.

"That's not a place where my uncle could easily get hold of it when he wanted it."

"But maybe the cistern would be the easiest, in case he was in a hurry. Maybe he knew the key wouldn't be of any value after a short time, anyway," Nelson argued.

Ted grinned in the faint light. "We've got a lot of explanations, but every one of them has something wrong with it. I guess the only thing we can do is search the barn."

"If that bozo out there hasn't beaten us to it," Nelson reminded them. "Well, if you birds are too chicken to help me look out there now, we may as well go back to bed. I guess that's what Condor has done, and he may be smarter than we are."

Neither Ted nor Marty cared to be thought less brave than Nelson, but they agreed that even if there was someone out in the barn, there would be little chance of finding him in the dark.

"And I don't think he's likely to find the key—or whatever he's looking for—in the dark, either," Marty observed.

Next morning they examined the bolts, but found them undisturbed, nor had any effort been made to force one of the windows. Evidently no attempt had been made to enter the house again. Marty went out to tend to the milking, and when he returned to the house for breakfast he looked puzzled.

"Say, Nel, you didn't sneak out and milk one of the cows again, did you?"

"Again? I never did it the first time. What's the matter?"

"One of them was dry. The other two were all right."

"Then there *was* somebody in the barn, and he must have stayed all night," Ted decided.

"And maybe he's still there!" said Nelson excitedly.

"Not very likely," was Marty's verdict. "Tramps often sneak in for a night's sleep, and may help themselves to milk or eggs or whatever they can get. But they're usually on their way again at the crack of dawn. Well, let's eat, and then we'll give that barn the best going over we can manage."

After a hearty though somewhat hurried breakfast, the boys started out for the barn. They began upstairs, and looking around at the immense room, with its big lofts partly filled with hay, Ted and Nelson realized what a job they had taken on. How could they hope to find anything as small as a key in all that space? There were hundreds of small nooks where a key could be easily secreted. And if it was under the hay, they had practically no chance at all of finding it, unless they pitched every forkful into the room below which was impossible.

"Well, I think about all we can do is cover some of the more obvious places," said Ted dubiously.

"I'm going to look for a key hanging on a wall right in plain sight," Nelson asserted.

"And I'm going to assume it isn't a key we're after, but something larger, and quite different," was Marty's approach to their problem. He picked up a pitchfork.

"What are you going to do with that?" asked Ted curiously.

"Go up in the lofts and poke around," Marty returned firmly.

"Good idea," Nelson agreed, and promptly picked up a pitchfork himself. "This will be good for finding something large hidden in the hay—like a man."

Although not taking a pitchfork with him, Ted followed the others up the ladder and into the loft. They were just about to begin what Nelson called Operation Pitchfork, when a voice from somewhere in the dark recesses of the loft halted them. They turned to see a man rising out of the hay, brushing the clinging wisps from his clothes and his hair.

Neither Ted nor Nelson had seen the man before, but they immediately suspected his identity. "Talk about your quiet farms," Nelson muttered. "This place is about as restful as Cape Canaveral."

It was Marty who pushed forward for a closer look.

"Why—it's the man in the blue Pontiac, isn't it? Are you Grover Hale?"

"That's right. And you're Marty Blaine, aren't you? I heard your newspaper friends call you that. Glad to see you again. Well, I suppose there's no way to keep out the press—or any great harm, either—though I did hope to see you alone."

"What for?" Marty demanded.

"For an alibi. Mind if we climb down out of here, where we can talk a little better?"

The others agreed, and they filed down to the main floor of the room. Hale was a little younger than they had expected, and seemed more cheerful than they would have expected a person in such deep trouble to be.

"Enjoy your milk?" Nelson asked of him.

"Yes, I did, and I'm sorry to say that's the only breakfast I've had. I'm not broke but I'm afraid to step into any public place and buy myself some food."

"How did you manage to avoid the police so far?" Ted inquired. "How did you get down here?"

Hale managed a half-humorous wink. "This is my regular vacation. Can I help it if I went to a remote fishing spot, with no radio or newspapers, and didn't know that the police were looking for me?"

"That won't do. Too many people know you didn't go."

"Yes, I suppose so. I'm not going to tell you all of the truth, because part of it involves another person who has nothing whatever to do with this matter. For personal reasons he doesn't want his name in the papers."

"You mean your friend on Callinger Road?"

"Oh, you know about that?" Hale looked annoyed. "Well, I'd better not say whether it is or it isn't. Anyway, I obviously couldn't drive around in my car, or even make personal inquiries myself, so my friend helped me out. He was the one who brought me down here. Marty, here, had dropped some hints in the little conversation I had with him at the curb in Forestdale, and my friend knew the reputations of Ted and Nelson whose trail I have managed to follow. I came down to this general area, and then inquired for a young newspaper reporter, and this is where I ended up."

"But why?" asked Marty.

"To make sure of something." Hale turned squarely upon him. "Do you recognize me as the man you saw at the curb last Saturday, and with whom you had a little talk?"

"Of course I do. There's no doubt about it."

"And you'd swear to that in court?"

"If I had to, yes."

Hale sighed with relief. "Well, then, that helps. I don't mean it'll clear me, but the way things look I'm going to need every point in my favor."

"You mean you *didn't* take that money?" Nelson demanded.

Hale turned upon him. "Whether I did or not, I would still answer that question 'no,' wouldn't I? That's why it's useless to deny an accusation. Build the kind of reputation you can stand on, and let it go at that—that's all you can do. And I thought I had."

"But a lot of people who were considered honest have embezzled money," Ted pointed out to him.

"Yes, unfortunately it's true—and most of these people are the kind who hate to swat a fly or catch a mouse in a trap. I can't explain it, except that handling such large quantities of money sort of leads to a contempt for it. Anyway, I didn't take that money."

"What's this alibi you want me to give you?" asked Marty.

"As I said, it isn't very much of an alibi, but it might help a little. At what time did you see me in Forestdale?"

"My bus pulled in at four o'clock, so it must have been about fifteen minutes after that."

"Fine!" He turned to Nelson. "You seem to be the most experienced driver around here. Could I go from Stanton to Forestdale in two hours?"

"Not in a car."

"Well, I went in my car. And I challenge anybody to make the trip in anything like that short a time. You'd end up with a dozen tickets for speeding, and probably wrap your car around a telephone pole besides."

"What good does that do you?" Ted asked.

"Just this. The theory of the police seems to be that I knew the bank examiner was coming in, so I fled. But the bank examiner only came in around two o'clock or so—their visits are never announced in advance—so I *didn't* leave for that reason. I took my normal leave, and went off on my vacation. I'm sure Marty will tell you that when I talked with him in Forestdale I looked more like a man on vacation than a fugitive from justice."

"That's right." Marty nodded his head.

"I wasn't trying to hide from anybody. I didn't know a thing about it, until I heard the late news Saturday night. Of course it was hard to decide what to do, but I happened to remember about Marty, and thought if I could find him, his evidence would be helpful. My friend agreed, although he also thought I should turn myself in as soon as possible."

"Now that you've found him, do you intend to do that?" asked Ted.

"I'll have to think it over, Ted. There are a few things I have to figure out. It's obvious that they have a pretty good case against me, and that means evidence must have been planted."

"Who could have done that?" asked Nelson.

"Oh, almost anybody at the bank, I guess. Well, is there any objection to a little breakfast, or am I beyond the pale?"

"You'll get your breakfast, all right," Marty assured him.

Hale looked at Ted.

"And you won't call the police—at least not right away?"

"No, I guess not," Ted pledged slowly. "I'm sure it would be better for your case if you'd turn yourself in instead of having somebody else do it."

"And I could have delayed you at least another hour or so," said Hale with a laugh, "although I didn't exactly relish having a pitchfork in my interior."

"What about last night?" asked Nelson. "Was there anybody else in the barn besides you?"

"Not that I know of."

"Then you just arrived last night?" asked Ted.

"Why, yes, around one o'clock, I think. Why?"

"Perhaps we'd better explain that after you eat," Ted returned. "We've got a long story to tell, too."

On the way to the house, Nelson managed to whisper to Ted: "Are we on safe ground, harboring a fugitive like this?"

"As far as I know, there's no warrant out for Hale's arrest. He could be just a man on a vacation that the police want to question."

"Does that make enough difference?"

"I hope so. We'll rely on it for a little while, but I'm sure Hale will have to make some kind of decision about it pretty soon."

CHAPTER 16

WAYS AND MEANS

THE CONDEMNED MAN ate a hearty meal," said Hale with a laugh, as he passed his plate for some more sausages.

The conversation proved rather lively. Ted saw no harm in acquainting Hale with some of the mysterious happenings at Meadows in the last few days. Hale was interested, but it was clear to everyone that he was so involved with his own affairs he could have played no part in the doings on the farm. Ted could tell, from some of Nelson's questions, that he had not given up hope of finding the missing bank money somewhere on the farm. But Ted was not so much concerned with where it could be, as why it would be there. Who had brought it? Surely not Hale. Even if he were guilty, he would have had no reason to bring it to Meadows.

Hale went on to describe the affairs of the bank in more detail than the newspapers had done.

"There's one thing that never came out in the papers," he continued, "but I don't know whether it will help me or hurt. I said I left the bank at my regular time—that would be between one and one-thirty, depending on how long it took me to balance my records. But I haven't told anyone—and apparently no one else noticed—that after I left the bank I went back. Actually I had forgotten my fountain pen. Now I know people might think it's not a very good reason for driving back after you're well on your way. But it's a fifteen-dollar pen, and furthermore I'd got used to it—that's important to a person who writes all day—and I didn't want anybody else using it, or possibly walking off with it. When I returned to my booth, I found that somebody had been at my window during my absence. That wouldn't be unusual during the time the window was open to the public, but this was after hours. Then I found this little piece of adding machine tape."

He took a slip of white paper from his pocket and unfolded it before them. It ran:

.00 *

11.14

12.27

3.26

5.07

6.27

38.01 *

"I had no particular reason for saving it," he went on, "except that if somebody had gone into my stall when he wasn't supposed to, I'd have something to prove it. There's not exactly any rule against it, but we're a little fussy about our own property, and there are plenty of adding machines scattered through a bank."

"Do the amounts mean anything to you?" asked Ted.

"Not particularly. Still, if I could find those exact numbers on somebody else's records it might help. But that's really looking for a needle in a haystack. A customer might have come in and paid five utility bills—say a gas bill, a fight bill, a water bill, a telephone bill, and a sewer tax—and this would be the total."

"I thought the bank was closed," Nelson reminded him.

"Yes, but one of the other tellers, or a bookkeeper, might have just added them up again, trying to check his records. I saved it as a little evidence for bawling somebody out for using my stuff, but now I think it might turn out to be more important than that. I didn't find it on my adding machine, somebody had torn it off and stuck it into my drawer. Either it was just an absent-minded little gesture, or it is very important."

"But there's no way you're likely to find out who it was?" asked Ted.

Hale shook his head. "No, I don't think so."

"Do you mind if I copy these figures down?"

"Be my guest."

Ted made the notations in his notebook, and returned the tape to Hale.

"Just how do you go about robbing a bank from the inside?" asked Nelson in some perplexity. "I can see how you could walk into a bank with a gun and make the teller hand over his cash, but I don't know how you would rob it otherwise."

"It's a little different from ordinary stealing," Hale explained, "because embezzling means you had a legal right to hold the property, but that you misused that right. You violated a trust by using other people's property to your own advantage. There are only two basic ways of doing this: one, you take the property and hope that it won't be missed; or two, you juggle the bookkeeping records so that a shortage will not be readily noticed.

"An embezzler has to use the possibilities within his own work. If he has access to the vaults where money or securities are kept, he may help himself to some of these, usually hoping to replace them before the loss is discovered. When a bank examiner comes into a bank—always unexpectedly—he must make sure that if the bank's records show there is so much money in the vaults, and so many notes and securities, that it is all there. He must also make sure that the bank is keeping its records in the manner prescribed by law, and that the books are in balance. In some ways it is very difficult for persons with access to the vaults, usually the officers, to help themselves because this is the sort of thing the examiner watches for. On the other hand, it is not easy to ask questions of high officials in the bank, and they are not so readily suspected.

"Embezzling by lesser employees is much more common. A bookkeeper who never handles cash or securities finds it pretty difficult to embezzle anything, unless he works with someone else, and embezzlers are notoriously lone hands. In small banks a person may act both as bookkeeper and teller, which would make the job of embezzlement considerably easier. But a teller can embezzle, even without the aid of a bookkeeper. He either puts deposit money into his own pocket and fails to send the slip to the bookkeeper to enter, or he forges withdrawal slips and puts the money into his own pocket.

"An embezzling teller leads a very uneasy life. His great problem is that the passbook of the depositor doesn't show the same balance as that shown on the bank's records. If a depositor comes in to withdraw a thousand dollars while his account at the bank shows a smaller figure, the teller must make sure he gets his thousand dollars, and covers the item by subtracting it from someone else's account. So he is faced with a constant juggling act among different customers. He must be sure he is never late to work, never absent, never on vacation; he probably brings his lunch for fear the depositor will be assisted by some other teller. He must know something about his depositors, too—what days they are likely to come in, how much they are likely to withdraw.

"There is an additional hazard in the annual audit. Some banks send a notice to each depositor giving the amount of his balance. If the teller is short, he tries to replace the money before the audit. The only other thing he can do is pretend the depositor has closed out his account completely, so he won't get a statement at all—a depositor may notice a *wrong* statement, but probably won't notice he failed to receive a statement. This works out very well—unless the depositor happens to walk into the bank unexpectedly some day.

"It's a tough racket, but oddly enough a teller doesn't have too much to fear from the bank examiner, though of course he can never be sure and is always uneasy when the examiner comes in. The examiner can't verify every depositor's account, and as long* as the teller has the cash on hand that the bank records say he ought to have, he will probably be all right. The records are wrong, but this is difficult to prove unless the teller is first suspected and then watched closely."

"Does it pay?" asked Nelson.

"In cash? Yes, you can get away with a certain amount of cash for a while. But is it worth living that way—always worrying? I believe that in the long run one is almost certain to be caught. If there is anything certain, it is that uncertain things will happen. What about that one day in a thousand when he can't get down to his job, or a depositor unexpectedly returns from a world cruise or any one of a hundred other things?

"There is another peculiar hazard about embezzling. Suppose you rob a bank with a gun, and you aren't caught within a few months. You're getting safer all the time. And if enough time passes, the probability is that you won't be caught at all. But an embezzler always has something hanging over his head if he doesn't replace the money. He may be caught five or ten or twenty years later."

"Doesn't the statute of limitations mean you are clear if you aren't caught within a certain period of time?" Ted inquired.

"On an ordinary robbery, yes. But remember that an embezzler has to keep juggling his records, and every time he makes a false entry he commits a new crime or renews the old one."

Hale had a favor to ask of Marty. "Would you be willing to give me a signed statement about what happened between us last Saturday? I know you're from out of the state, and it might be difficult for me to locate you when I need you."

"Of course," Marty readily agreed. "We can use my uncle's typewriter. Let's write it now."

With Marty and Hale so occupied, Ted and Nelson went outside again.

"What now, Ted? The barn again?"

"No, I don't think so. I've lost my confidence about finding anything useful there. This sure is a tough business, hunting for something when you don't know what it is."

"Or why you're hunting for it," Nelson added. "But I'm still fascinated by that old cistern, Ted. When a man will stay out in a driving rainstorm to fool around with it, it must be important. The way I figure it, maybe Mr. Martin didn't *know* the key was so valuable, and so he just tossed it away. Mr. Hauser knows what it's for, and so he's anxious to get it."

"Still, the cistern would be a strange place to toss it. No, there's got to be another explanation why a man in a rainstorm. . . . Hey!" he called suddenly.

"What's up?"

"I wonder if those footprints have somehow fooled us and aren't telling us what we think they are."

"You mean that maybe Mr. Hauser walked *backwards* to the cistern?"

"No, that didn't occur to me—because then how did he get away again? We were still making footprints in that mud the next morning. But there's something that sort of sticks in my mind. Marty went to meet Mr. Hauser in the sugar house the next morning. Now if Mr. Hauser had been out in that heavy rain, what about his clothes?

Marty didn't mention it, so maybe there wasn't anything unusual about his clothes."

"What about a change of clothes?"

"You'd hardly think he'd bring along a change of clothes on an errand like this, would you? He probably couldn't have known in advance that he was going to get caught in the rain. And he couldn't dry and press his clothes at the sugar house. Now if all this is true, then he *wasn't* out in the rain."

"Then where was he—at the bottom of the cistern? He'd get wet there, too."

"Yes, there's always that cistern. And I'm beginning to get the idea that the cistern is the missing clue we need."

"Think we ought to get it pumped out?"

"We can't without Mrs. Martin's permission, and anyway it would take too long. But can't we explore it ourselves?"

"You mean go down into the water ourselves? How deep do you think it is?"

"I don't have any idea, but we could ask Mrs. Martin. I think she'd agree to let us try it. She's been upset by these happenings, too."

Mrs. Martin was working in the kitchen when they went in. Marty and Hale had gone into the study to type up their statement, and the sound of the typewriter could be heard through the closed door. The boys quickly explained their project to Mrs. Martin.

"The water's only about four feet deep," she told them, "although I don't know what good it will do you, splashing around in all that slime. Are you sure you want to do it?"

"I think it is worth a trial," Ted said.

"Yes," Nelson added, "and in case nothing else comes of it, he can always write a newspaper story about 'My First Trip Down a Cistern.' "

"Well, you'll need some different clothes. I'll find you some old things, and there's a pair of high rubber boots around. You'll find a strong rope out in the barn, and tie it carefully around you. You'd better wait till Marty's done, and there'll be two to hold you."

"Oh, I can manage by wrapping the rope around something," Nelson assured her.

"Nelson has never let me down yet," Ted stated.

He changed clothes, and they found the rope. Removing the top from the cistern was an easy job, and Ted was soon ready to make his descent. He eased over the edge, and gradually lowered himself down as Nelson continued to let out the little play in the rope. Nelson's legs were braced, the rope wrapped around a tree, and Ted knew that he would not let go of that rope if his life depended on it.

"My First Trip Down a Cistern" might not make such a bad newspaper story after all, Ted decided. Certainly it was an eerie experience. By looking up he could see the empty sky overhead; around him he was closed in by walls; below him was that foreboding water with green scum floating on top, and nobody-knew-what swimming around inside it. Below that was the mud. Ted didn't exactly relish the idea of squashing around in it, with the water overflowing the top of his boots, but it couldn't be helped. He wondered if he would ever feel clean again, and decided he wouldn't until he had soaked for two hours in a warm bath at home.

Actually he had no plans, other than to get down in the cistern to see what might have been of such interest to Mr. Hauser.

A kind of ledge jutted out about six feet down, on which Ted rested his feet for a moment. Then he slid off and down, past the ledge. It was very dark down there, and he wondered if he would be able to see. His head was beyond the ledge now, and just under it the darkness seemed complete. But his eyes gradually accommodated themselves so that he could see a little better than at first, and he saw . . .

What was it? He could hardly be sure. But staring at it in the gloom he gradually became convinced that he was looking at a yawning hole, like the entrance to a long tunnel.

CHAPTER 17

THE TALKING ROOM

HE COULDN'T explore the tunnel now. His rope would not reach far enough and he had no light.

"Hey, Nel!"

"Yeah?"

"Pull me up!"

"So soon? You didn't even get your feet wet."

"I know, and I'm not going to. Heave up!"

Obligingly, Nelson pulled up on the rope, which was more difficult than letting it down, but in a few minutes Ted was back on solid earth again.

"Well, what?" Nelson demanded.

"There's a tunnel leading off below there. You can't see it from above. Remember what Mr. Crowell was telling us about the Underground Railroad? I'll bet that's where slaves were hidden. That tunnel's probably been there for over a hundred years, and the Martins never even guessed it. Now we know why Mr. Hauser didn't get wet in the rain. He was down in that tunnel!"

"A tunnel! Boy, I wonder where it leads to?"

"It goes into the house."

"Then when we heard those footsteps, Mr. Hauser was really in the house and not in the house at the same time. But I wonder what he was after. Could it be the bank money?"

"I don't see how it could, unless he put it there himself. I doubt if anyone else knew about the tunnel. And while it might be a good place to hide something, it would be pretty difficult to get to. Anyway, he never had any connection with the bank."

"Well, we've still got to get into that tunnel and explore it. Want me to try?"

"Why not me? I'm dressed for it."

"But you didn't even get muddy."

Marty appeared just then.

"Say, what are you doing? Aunt Karen said something about your going down the cistern, but she couldn't imagine why. Did you find anything?"

"I'll say we did," Nelson burst out. "Just a secret tunnel, leading under the house."

"A tunnel? Now who in the world would think of something like that?"

"There were certain people who *weren't* supposed to think of it— slavecatchers who were after escaping slaves. That was about as safe a place as you could imagine."

"Where's Hale?" Ted suddenly asked Marty.

"Oh, we finished with the statement, and he said he wanted to think it over for a little while. I thought he was just going to take a little stroll outside. But he went down to the road, and suddenly a car pulled up, he got in and it drove off. I didn't have a chance to get the license number. I didn't even get a good look at the car—the hedge cut off part of the view."

"How about that?" Nelson exclaimed. "Maybe we just helped a suspected criminal escape."

After examining the cistern from the top, Marty said that he believed they could put a long ladder down into the cistern, and from there could swing themselves over to the tunnel entrance. Although all three of them could have gone down, it was decided that Marty at least ought to stay out, just in case something went wrong. The ladder was lowered, and provided with flashlights, the other two descended with Ted in the lead.

When Ted's head had cleared the jutting ledge, and his feet had nearly touched the murky water of the cistern, he flashed his light around. Everything was about the way he would have expected the interior of a cistern to be—with one exception. Just below the ledge, and a number of feet above the level of the water, was a large circular opening. It led into a well-constructed tunnel of brick. Probably the ledge itself had been deliberately constructed to hide the tunnel entrance from above. Ted flashed his light down the tunnel, but the beam did not carry very far.

A board going from a step of the ladder to the edge of the tunnel would have been useful, but Ted decided he could get along without it. He managed to swing himself from the ladder to the tunnel, then crouched inside waiting for Nelson to join him. Then they started down the low tunnel, flashing their lights ahead of them.

"I used to enjoy exploring sewers when I was a kid," said Nelson with a grunt, as he bumped his head once or twice against the top, although he was bending over about as far as he could and still walk. Had the tunnel been slightly smaller, they would have been obliged to crawl.

As they thought, the tunnel led directly under the house, and took them almost exactly to its center. Above them they could see the floor supports of the first-story rooms. A very steep ladder led up from the tunnel, and climbing this they passed the first floor of the house. Another ladder led them past the second floor, and to a trap door. Opening this, they climbed up into a small attic room.

There was absolutely no other window or door in the room, and the air was musty and the dust a century thick. They coughed a little, but since the walls of the room were loosely constructed and there was some communication up the shaft, they were able to breath without too much discomfort.

They flashed their fights about. There was some makeshift old furniture, a mattress, some old clothing practically in shreds and an old safe.

"Wow!" Nelson exclaimed. "Then there really was a key missing, and now we know what it was for. Notice those prints in the dust, Ted? Somebody was here not very long ago. It must have been Mr. Hauser. He thought Marty might be able to find the key lying around the house. I wonder how Mr. Hauser knew about the tunnel?"

"Remember Mr. Crowell said that Mr. Hauser may have overheard part of the conversation with Mr. Martin? He must have learned enough to give him some ideas, and Mr. Crowell had all those old Civil War books where he could look things up. Mr. Hauser probably always watched for a chance to make a profit on something."

"But what did he expect to find in that safe? It couldn't be the bank's money, could it?"

"Hardly. We might as well forget about that money, Nel. We're never going to find it. Either Hale or somebody else at the bank took it, and they've got it stashed away somewhere, invested in something else or they lost it gambling. Anyway this safe hasn't been opened in years, I'll bet."

"But there might be money in it—old time money. It would still be good, wouldn't it? It wouldn't be Confederate money if it was used to help the runaway slaves. I wonder why they needed a safe up here?"

"I suppose they had to give money to the slaves and the people who helped them, and maybe tickets and papers, too. I suppose you can't trust everybody."

"But how did they get that old safe up here? It's too big to be dragged through that tunnel."

"They must have brought it up while they were building the house, and then sealed this room off from the rest of the house. Just think of the stories this room could tell if it could only talk. Listen, let's not stay here too long. The air's pretty bad, and we'll have to figure out what to do about that safe."

Nelson had examined the ancient container and was satisfied there was no way for them to open it. Even the lock might have been rusted and useless, in case they had the right key to open it.

"All right, let's go, Ted. But we'll be back."

They retraced their steps, and soon reached the top of the cistern again.

"I can't have you boys going through there again," Mrs. Martin decided when they had told her and Marty of their find. "It's too risky, and the air is too bad. But just think, that secret room was there all these years and we never suspected it. If you know exactly where it is, perhaps we could knock a hole through the ceiling and reach it that way."

Both Ted and Nelson remembered having seen the chimney running along one side of the room, and with this as a guide they were able to tell where the secret room could be reached from one of the bedrooms. Nelson and Marty started to knock a hole through the ceiling, later to be fitted with a trap door while Ted drove off in Nelson's car, determined to locate a locksmith.

By the time he returned with one, the hole was big enough for the four of them to climb into the room above. There the locksmith set about his work, and within half an hour had the door of the safe swinging open on its rusty hinges.

If Nelson had expected to find any money, he was disappointed. But the safe was full of old books and ledgers and diaries and letters. Ted was elated.

"This looks like a real find. Be sure to handle everything carefully; some of this stuff is ready to fall apart. Why, this one seems to be an account of this station in the Underground Rail-road. Remember how I said I wished this room could talk? Well, it seems to be talking, telling its whole history. I'll bet Mr. Dobson will be eager to look at some of this."

"Do you think he could use it?" asked Marty.

"If it's what I think it is, he could. The newspaper would be able to print excerpts from some of this material. Of course the *Town Crier* space rates are quite low, but I'm sure he'd be willing to copyright the material in your aunt's name. Then perhaps some future use could be made of it. Mr. Crowell might give us some advice about that."

"Do you think Mr. Hauser knew this stuff was here?" asked Nelson.

"Maybe not exactly, but he was able to guess there was something pretty valuable locked up in that old safe. Maybe he expected some money, too. But I'm certain that this material does have a strong historical value, and it might have a financial value, besides."

"Well, anything that will help my aunt out would mean a good deal," Marty remarked. "She's always had to watch her money so carefully."

Mrs. Martin readily gave her permission for Ted to take the documents along with him. Ted put through a long-distance call to Mr. Dobson, who said he would be glad to look at the material, and, if it turned out to be what he expected, to use some of it.

"But there was one more thing," Ted mentioned more to Nelson than to the others. "Grover Hale has just turned himself in."

"That's not surprising," Marty put in. "I knew he was seriously considering it."

"Yes, but that's not all. He turned himself over to *Ken Kutler*, and it's Kutler who's got the inside story."

"That was mean," said Nelson determinedly. "After all, you had a chance to call the police, and you didn't. Now Ken will get all the credit."

"Well, the way Mr. Dobson talked, I gathered that Ken had worked hard on the story. He had somehow heard about Hale's friend on Callinger Road, and located him, and through him was trying to persuade Hale to turn himself in. This happened before Hale ever came down here."

"That paper Marty signed probably made him decide," said Nelson.

"What about this story right here, Ted?" asked Marty.

"Well, I suppose these documents are the real story, and no doubt Mr. Dobson will publish a short account of how they were found. But I don't think I got anywhere on the story I came down here to get—even though I did meet Grover Hale. That's the way the wishbone breaks."

"You helped my aunt out, too," Marty reminded him. "That's something, isn't it? If it hadn't been for you, she might have sold her farm and turned her money over to this phony. Maybe that isn't a headline story, but it means the world to us."

"Yes, Ted, what's going to happen to Mr. Hauser? Have we got him for anything?"

"He stole two hundred dollars from Mrs. Martin, but these papers should be worth more than that, and we wouldn't have found them if it hadn't been for him. I imagine she can just forget about that money. It would be hard to collect, anyway. But Mr. Hauser's lost his job. And he's got a crooked hip to live with for the rest of his life."

"He's got something worse than a crippled hip. He's got a crippled mind."

There was nothing further to detain Ted and Nelson at Meadows so they packed up and were soon ready to leave.

"Just one thing, Marty," said Nelson as they left their bedroom with the new opening in the ceiling and started toward the stairs. "Why was your suitcase so heavy? Ted and I had quite a powwow over that."

Marty laughed. "I didn't know that was part of the mystery. Come on, and I'll show you."

They followed him into his bedroom, where he pulled the suitcase out from under the bed, unlocked it, and threw back the cover. Then they saw what had made it so heavy. There in the case were eight or ten thick, heavy, college textbooks.

"I have some studying to do over the summer," Marty explained. "So you see why I didn't want to borrow any of your books, Ted. I already had plenty of my own."

CHAPTER 18

THE TAPE

IN SPITE of all the excitement both boys felt let-down as they approached Forestdale—for after all, they *had* failed in their chief mission. Ted fingered his notebook listlessly, while Nelson's attention was on the road.

"If only that tape Hale found really *did* mean something," he mused.

"Forget it, Ted. You don't even know how things work in a bank. If it did have any meaning, there'd be no way for you to figure it out. But the chances are it's just an old piece of adding machine tape that doesn't mean anything at all."

"Well, I do know a *little* bit about bookkeeping, Nel. I often enter the day's expenses in the cash book for Mr. Dobson. And if I'm around at the right time I make up the daily deposit slip, too. First I type the date of each check, and then the amount . . ."

He stared down at his notebook. He had been doodling with his pencil, and an idea suddenly struck him.

"Say, Nel, stop the car and look at this. What do you think it means?"

"What's the use of looking? I couldn't figure it out in a month of Sundays, Mondays, Tuesdays . . ."

"Well, look anyway."

Nelson parked on the side of the road and glanced at the paper. He saw what Ted had done with the figures. They now read:

```
          .00 *
         11/14
         12/27
          3/26
          5/07
          6/27

        38.01 *
```

"Why, that looks like November 14, December 27, March 26, May 7—and June 27. Well, what about it?"

"Because June 27 was the last day the bank examiner called. What if all these dates were the times when the bank examiner was expected?"

"That's crazy, Ted. Nobody knows ahead of time when a bank examiner is coming in."

"But suppose somebody did? I noticed that it was a rather dirty and ragged piece of tape, folded quite a few times. I know Hale had been carrying it around in his pocket for a few days, but it seemed too old even for that. Only I didn't think of it till now."

Nelson looked at it again. "What does the total mean, then?"

"Nothing, I suppose. It was just a total of the dates, to make it look like a normal piece of addition. Somebody wanted to keep a list of the dates, and put it on an adding machine tape which would seem perfectly innocent around a bank. I've got to show this to Mr. Dobson. Let's get going."

Mr. Dobson, shoving the Civil War documents aside until he could examine them later, listened carefully to Ted's story.

"It's an interesting idea, Ted. And I think it's very easily verified."

He put through a call to Stanton, and in a few minutes had the information he desired.

"You're right, Ted. Those *are* the dates the bank examiner called. Of course it is possible that someone made up this tape on or after June 27, but if the tape was as old as you think, that would rule out that probability."

"What are we going to do with the story, Mr. Dobson? We don't know the real answer."

"No," said the editor grimly, "but we know the right questions to ask. I'm revising tomorrow's front page. This will be our feature story—under your by-line. We'll simply print the information, and ask the proper officials what explanation *they've* got for it."

"But who's the guilty one?" asked Nelson. "Could it be Grover Hale after all?"

"I doubt it. He would never have showed this tape to Ted, if he knew it could be so incriminating. For of course it might incriminate him as much as anyone."

"Maybe that's exactly what he was figuring on, and he was playing it real cool."

"I don't think so, Nelson. People can't do too much acting in real life because if they act out of character, those who know them get suspicious. Besides, it would have to involve someone higher up than Grover Hale."

"You mean an officer of the bank?" asked Ted.

"Someone even higher up than that. Who knows when a bank examiner is coming in? Nobody, except *the bank examiner himself*. And now, Ted, let's get to work on that story."

* * * *

Ted's story did, indeed, touch off an explosion in the proper political and financial circles, not to mention a swell of public interest. As the evidence was uncovered, it became clear that Grover Hale was innocent. It was the president of the bank and the bank examiner who had been involved in a deal. Important securities which were supposedly in the locked vaults of the bank had been removed and used as collateral for other investments. It was necessary for the president to know when the bank examiner was coming so he could make arrangements since the examiner always had an assistant or two with him. If there had been something the assistants were forbidden to look into, suspicions would have been aroused.

Although Grover Hale was innocent and honest, his records were *not* honest. The president had set up a dummy account, which Hale handled, thinking it was a legitimate account. Then the money was stolen again. If the shortage was discovered, there would be evidence to make Hale look like the guilty party.

The scheme had succeeded until the bank examiner learned June 27 was to be his last visit, after which he would be transferred to another district. Because his successor would surely discover the shortage, the examiner had to seem to make the discovery of the shortage himself.

Since the president did not explain, it was never known exactly how the incriminating tape got into Hale's drawer. One theory was that the president realized the shortage would be discovered, and wanted to indicate a conspiracy between Hale and the bank examiner. Another theory was that he dropped it accidentally when he went into Hale's drawer for some forms he needed to further incriminate the teller.

"Why would a bank examiner stoop to something like this?" asked Nelson, when they were discussing the case later.

"He had a chance to make ten times his annual salary. What would you have done?"

"I guess I would have been tempted," Nelson admitted. "Only I'm lucky. I wouldn't think I was smart enough to get away with it. This case was full of spooky moments wasn't it, right up to the last minute coming into Forestdale when you were moaning that you hadn't done anything in the case. And all the time you had the answer right in your notebook."

"As far as I'm concerned, the spookiest thing was the way nine different and presumably reliable witnesses claimed that Marty had been riding with Grover Hale—and it never happened. Doesn't it make you think?"

"I guess it would, if anything could." Nelson laughed. "Well, what next, Ted?"

"Just let me dream about this for a while. By-lines, reporters calling me, getting quoted in papers all over the state. What more do I need?"

"Nothing right now." Nelson laughed. "But wait till the next good lead comes in. You'll forget all about this case and be off on your next big story."

www.ingramcontent.com/pod-product-compliance
Lightning Source LLC
Chambersburg PA
CBHW020657180626
46816CB00003B/1330